A WICKED EDUCATION

A STUDY HARD ROMANCE

MIKA LANE

HEADLANDS PUBLISHING

COPYRIGHT

Copyright© 2022 by Mika Lane
Headlands Publishing
4200 Park Blvd. #244
Oakland, CA 94602

ISBN ebook 978-1-948369-82-4
ISBN print 978-1-948369-83-1

BE THE FIRST TO KNOW...

Want more heat, heart,
and bad boys who know what they're doing?
Join my list and I'll send the steam straight to your inbox,
starting with a deliciously naughty story:

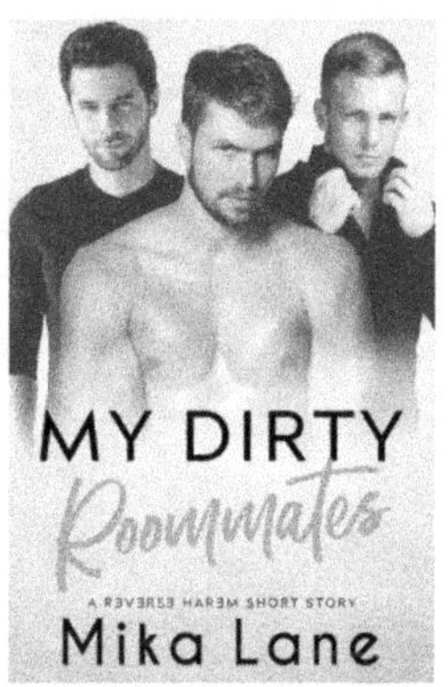

1

JESSA CARR

"So anyway, it was super hot—like eighty-five degrees —when Stephanie, Melanie, Brandie and I arrived in PV. You know?"

Yeah. I knew.

How could I *not* know that Tiffanie from down the hall had just gotten back from Puerto Vallarta for spring break?

Or 'PV,' as she called it. Like she was a regular there or something. Where it was hot and sunny and beautiful and everyone got great tans.

She'd only been talking about 'PV' since the beginning of the semester. So yeah, I knew.

Her bubbly enthusiasm, as much as it chafed me, was a distraction of sorts from the hubbub swirling around our dorm. The hubbub that I was not part of. While it was always like this on 'return days,' when people got back to school after a long break, today it was more like a bomb had gone off. After all, spring break was the most revered break of the entire school year.

And after two and a half years at Wellshire University, I'd been able to sort the 'return days' into piles.

The first, and most chaotic, was move-in day, which happened twice a year—once in late August, and again in mid-January. This was, of course, at the start of each semester, when rooms may or may not be shuffled, new people were moving in and had no idea where to go, and everyone's crap was piled up on sidewalks as their parents unloaded and then took off before getting roped into carrying duffel bags and other junk into multi-floor walk ups built before the ADA had required elevators and ramps.

And if I were to rate those two move-in days, August was definitely worse because you were moving in everything you were bringing to school. At least over Christmas break, you could leave whatever you wanted to behind, making the January return a lot easier.

Yes, January move-in was mellower. That was when you'd have your winter starts. There were fewer newbies arriving, instead just returning students putting away whatever new electronics and the occasional winter sweater they'd scored as holiday gifts.

Today, though, was the most exciting of all return to campus days—the famed spring break return. Over holiday break, the weather was usually crappy and most people all went to the same place, namely home. Oh sure, some would go to a boyfriend's or girlfriend's home, and a very select few went on an exotic vacation like skiing or some such. But those were few and far between.

Spring break, though? Now that was exciting. It was the return when most people had gone somewhere and did stupid college shit they'd never tell their kids about, which kept campus gossip buzzing for days. It was the day when people screamed in excitement or cried in embarrassment.

Yes, there were always tears.

For me though, it was torture. At least this year.

For some of the girls in my dorm, my room had become a sort of gathering place. Part of it was because of my roommate, Birdie. She was just that sort of person who attracted lots of friends. She was sweet and sort of nerdy-cool. And while she spent most of her free time working in the library, she was also always willing to lend an ear to someone in need, whether it be some girl bellyaching over a boyfriend ghosting her, or a lousy grade when they thought they deserved better.

But Birdie wasn't there yet, not having arrived from her own romantic spring break with not one, but three hot dudes. Who happened to all be employed by the university. How she pulled that off still baffled me, but I had to say, I'd never seen my friend happier.

So that day, to my surprise, the passersby who stopped in were there to see *me*. I was the funky social boho girl, the Bettie Page lookalike who rocked corset tops and combat boots, went through eyeliner like some people went through toothpaste, and often had a sarcastic, occasionally insightful, and sometimes downright rude comment on everything.

I was an outlier in the world of beautiful, preppy Wellshire University blondes. But, for some unfathomable reason, people still liked me.

Which pissed me off from time to time. I mean, I'd spent a good part of my life being the 'alt chick' and making sure I was the most unpopular girl in school. Why college turned that on its head was beyond me. Unexpected, and not at all understood.

I turned my attention from the couple out in front of my dorm arguing so loudly they might have been right in my room, each accusing the other of cheating during their separate trips. Like I said, spring break ended, for some people, in tears.

From the stories I'd heard each year, this vacation rite of passage was about a lot of things, but fidelity was not one of them.

Tiffanie continued her debrief. Which I had not asked for.

She slammed her hands on her hips. "You would not believe how drunk Stephanie got that first night. Oh my god, she drank like, two gallons of margaritas. And you know how she gets."

"Not really," I muttered, feeling the headache behind my eyeballs increase in volume. Fuck all, where was Birdie? She'd rescue me from this drivel, smiling and nodding politely as she always did, patiently listening to Tiffanie share her download.

While I'd put in my earbuds and listen to music or a podcast.

"Well, Stephanie is like, a total slut when she gets drunk," Tiffanie continued. "So like, it's two in the morning and she's got like, three guys dancing with her, feeling her up, her left boob's out of her dress. I mean, it was like… damn girl, get you some!"

Tiffanie laughed, but part of me wanted to roll my eyes. The other part was a little jealous. I wasn't proud of that, but it was true. Party girl might not have come back from Mexico with a boyfriend, but at least she'd gotten some action. Better than my spring break.

"So what about you, what did you do?" she asked hopefully.

Before I could answer, another visitor, this time from the guys' floor, popped in. "As hot as Miami was," Charlie Conners said, giving both of us hungry looks, "I'd say the view is much better back here at Well*shit*."

We rolled our eyes. It was what you did with Charlie, grade-a horndog and supposed accounting major. But everyone knew what he really majored in was pussy. As in, he treated pussy like Pokémon. Gotta catch 'em and all that. But at least he was honest about it, not trying to pretend like he wanted a real relationship with his conquests.

I had to hand him that.

"*Really, Charlie?*" Tiffanie asked in pretend offense. I knew she was on his to-do list. Actually, he'd made it pretty clear I was on his to-do list too. I just wasn't interested.

I smiled, just to torment him a little. "Wow, Charlie, looks like you brought a nice tan home from Miami," I said, looking him over.

I'd bet that wasn't all he brought home, with the fucking around he probably did.

Ew.

It was no secret how busy the campus health center was after spring break.

Charlie grinned, flexing his biceps in his new Miami tank top. "You know it, Jessa. So, you ladies had a good spring break? Ready to study hard now? Only a couple months left in the semester you know," he said with a big grin, as if he ever studied.

"You're always studying *hard*, Charlie," I said, making Tiffanie laugh. "Too bad you don't study *long*."

"There's more than one way to study, oh Snow White vixen of the third floor," he said with a deep bow.

Accepting that I wasn't interested in his spiel, he turned all his focus to Tiffanie. "If I can ever share with you some of those alternative ways to study, Miss Tiff, I'm only a staircase away."

Tiffanie gave Charlie *the look*. I'd learned it pretty well since coming to campus. It was the look that said 'We can stop the conversation any time you want. Let's get down to fucking.'

Maybe that meant she'd get out of my hair.

But not yet. "You know Charlie, I *was* thinking about hitting the books tonight," she said with a twinkle, then turned to me. "But I was just asking Jessa here about her spring break. What did you do, girl?"

Charlie could not be less interested in my spring break, particularly when there was potential sex on the table.

And not wanting to cock-block the guy, I made it brief.

"Nothing as exciting as you two," I said, moving toward the door to get them out of my room before they started rutting on the carpet. "Went to wine country, did some artsy shit. That's all."

"Ah, wine country," Charlie said with a grin. "You know, Jessa, I'd love to see what kind of girl you are when you've got a bottle or two in you."

"Not gonna happen, Charlie," I told him for what felt like the hundredth time. "Besides, you and Tiffanie have some *studying* to do, right?"

"Always willing to do a *group session* if it includes you, Jessa," he said.

I had to give him credit for persistence.

He turned to Tiffanie, who'd already started fluffing her hair and pushing her boobs out. I didn't have the heart to tell her she didn't need to try so hard. Charlie was pretty much a sure thing. "Shall we?" he said gallantly.

It was funny, the sudden, almost gentlemanly question at the end of Charlie's blatant panty chasing, but Tiffanie was all for it. They went in one direction and I in the other to the vending machine, where I grabbed a pack of Twinkies

I tore them open like a starving animal and bit into the soft sponge cake, closing my eyes and savoring the greasy deliciousness. They were my kryptonite for so many reasons, and at that moment, the sugary sweetness was a welcome about-face from my own spring break. I did go to wine country, like I'd told Tiffanie and Charlie, but it wasn't on some single-woman get away, where I got dramatic vistas all day, drank wine all evening, and slept with hot, hunky vintners all night.

Nope, I went with my mother. That's right, Wellshire University's resident raven haired rockabilly chick went on spring break with Mommy. We *did* tour a bunch of vineyards, and I *did* get plenty of pics for great landscapes and interesting material to use later in my art classes. But instead of gallons of wine, I sipped and tasted tiny quantities of it in between bottles of spring water. Instead of rich, luxurious foods, we nibbled at vegetarian sample platters. Oh, and yoga. There was lots of yoga. Mom had turned the trip into a 'detox your body, detox your mind' tour.

It was the biggest bait and switch in the history of mother-daughter travel.

And I didn't see a single dick. I saw plenty of men, of course. And like just about everywhere else I'd gone since my boobs started growing from acorns into the size of grapefruits, I got plenty of interested looks.

But everyone kept their pants on, especially me. That's how things worked you travel with your very married, very protective mother. Three out of the five nights I couldn't even use the little vibrator I'd packed, since I had to share a room with Mom.

So, my friend the Twinkie was a lame act of rebellion, a silent protest against a week of endive, tahini, kale, and textured vegetable protein. I never thought I'd say this, but I was looking forward to the dining hall starting back up tomorrow. I was ready for burgers, fries, and fish sticks.

As I returned to my room, I navigated all the noise and attention. Three guys tried to start up conversations, clearly trying to get into my pants, but, no. Not gonna happen. Truth was, walking through the dorm, past the common room and up the stairs, I had to admit I was bored with boys.

I wanted a *man*.

Part of college life was, of course, about hooking up. Fact. I might not have been a psych or sociology major, but I knew that the instinctive drive to figure out what the hell you wanted to do in life, and who you wanted to do in life, was amplified by having so many options available as one does on a college campus.

For me though, I was done with the games and the silliness. Drunk frat bros who paid people to write their papers because they were too lazy or dumb. Minute men who barely lasted long enough to stick it in. Dumbasses who didn't even know how to do their own laundry.

I wanted to be *inspired*. I wanted to be *challenged*. I wanted to feel the same passion from a lover that I felt when I was painting or using my imagination. I wanted…

Well, something that Charlie and the other guys around campus didn't offer, that was for damn sure.

I got back to my room, closing the door to cut off the constant drop-ins. I just wasn't up for the stories of drunken debauchery that highlighted all that I hadn't done over spring break.

And didn't really want to do, anyway.

Instead I plugged my phone into my laptop to transfer all the photos I took, hoping that maybe I could find something inspirational for my next painting project. I had about three quarters of them done when my door opened again, and in walked my roommate.

Thank fucking god.

I threw my arms around her and stepped back.

What a difference a semester could make. Her entire freshman year, she was the hidden flower of Wellshire, absolutely gorgeous but so shy and reserved she was nearly invisible. And she was a virgin on top of all that.

More than once I wondered whether her shyness was just an act. With those big eyes, pouty full lips, tight body, and big, bouncy brown hair, she had no clue she was attractive. It was as if she'd never looked in a mirror. Damnedest thing.

Until last semester. After confessing to our friend Roxy and me that she was a virgin, and a joking comment on our part that she should use that as inspiration for an English class essay, her life changed, practically overnight.

And that's why my girl had just gotten back from spring break with her *three* boyfriends. Her three *older* boyfriends. Her three *older, professor* boyfriends. Maybe I was a little jealous.

But thrilled for her, too.

"How was your spring break, Jessa?" she asked with a tight hug.

"Eh. Boring," I said, hugging her just as tightly.

Geez, she looked amazing.

Was that what a week straight of fucking three hot guys did for you? If I could bottle that, I'd be one rich bitch.

Gone were Birdie's insecure glances, or the slightly confused looks as the sounds of college life filtered into our room. Instead a confident, beautiful, and sexy woman who knew the power of not just her mind but her spirit and sexuality, crossed the room to put her bag down on what was technically her university-issued dorm bed.

I say technically because most nights she no longer spent in our room. She slept at her mens' places, going to bed with one or more of them. And this past spring break was probably an erotic adventure that would have blown even my dirty imagination.

Not that I was above digging for details. "So? How was your week with the… guys?" I asked, jonesing for juicy details.

Guys. Multiple guys. More than one. And I'm not

talking a measly menage. These crazy kids were a foursome.

A goddamn *foursome*.

Who knew that was even a thing?

Jessa hadn't, either. Until it was.

Her new arrangement was something I still wasn't sure how to handle in public conversation. And while she was no longer in any of her lovers' classes, that didn't mean people didn't know things. And talk. So I did what I could to quell any rumors, since around Wellshire U, about the only thing more popular than sex was gossip.

"Everything was amazing," she sighed happily, falling back on the bed and stretching her arms above her head. "We went to the mountains, to Kai's family cabin, and… yeah, it was good."

I chuckled jealously at the way she said *good*. Such a bland word, but so full of possibility. "So are there any fantasies you didn't get fulfilled?" I asked, trying not to look desperate for a racy story.

Birdie gave me a look that had me burning inside, and her huge crooked grin could only be described as shit-eating. "Nope."

She was killing me. But I wasn't going to beg.

"Wow." I got up and locked the door.

If our friend Roxy came by, I'd let her in, but that was it. Everyone else could pound sand, including Tiffanie. Oh wait, Tiffanie was probably off having sex with Charlie Conners, so she wouldn't be by anytime soon, anyway. Unless he was a minute man.

Trying not to look too eager, I continued. "Okay, I've got to ask. In all your… time together, you've had a few, shall we say, group activities, right?"

Birdie rolled her eyes. "Of course. Do you think they line up outside my door and come in one at a time? Hello! I mean, we have one on ones sometimes, but normally it's at least two of the guys, and most of the time all three." Her eyes fell closed, and she smiled. "God. How did I get this life?"

I wondered that, too.

After a moment of dreamy remembering, she continued. "Like last week, I was in the hot tub with Leo when Cary walked in on us… and joined. It was so freaking hot. You have to try it sometime."

Um, yeah.

"I bet." I took a deep breath, repressing my own shivers at the image. Her guys Leo and Cary were *nice*, and I didn't mean personality-wise. "I was just think-ing, Birdie, have you ever, you know, sat back and watched as two of your men engaged in some sweaty naked wrestling?"

"Sweaty naked wrestling?" Birdie asked, laughing and shaking her head. "No. The guys are just into me. Not that I would mind seeing something like that. But it's not their thing."

"So you've… done everything with them, right?"

My previously innocent virgin roommate nodded. "Yup. Not a single virgin inch of flesh left here. We like to experiment from time to time. Keep things very… fresh."

"What do you mean?"

"Well, there was that time Kai lapped up my ass like it was a bowl of ice cream," she said with a big grin, shivering at the memory, "and in return I massaged his prostate, blowing him while sticking a finger up his backside."

Okay. My formerly virgin roommate had just surpassed me in sexual experience.

"Did he like it?" I asked in a croaky voice.

"His nickname is now Firehose," Birdie said, grinning. "Seriously, he came so hard his balls literally ached afterwards. You should have seen him walk. So... I'd say, yeah, we're open to trying *some* new things."

I sat back, flushed and almost sweating at the thought. "Fuuuuck. Daaaamn."

I just didn't have the words. Birdie had become a woman, and it showed. Even her hair was more gorgeous— still long and curly, but mature and sexy, with one sultry lock hanging over her eye, making her look like the temptress that she was. The confidence really stood out. And impressed me. Then again, if she'd been handling three dicks on the regular, no wonder she was more confident.

"Hey... I'm still me, remember?" Birdie said, almost reading my mind. She grinned, and tugged at one of her curls like she used to. "Really, Jessa."

"I know, I just... am very jealous of your spring break compared to mine."

She let out a relieved laugh, and sat back. "Okay, fill

me in. Last time we talked, you were going to wine country with your mom. Not my choice, but… okay."

"Yeah, shouldn't have been my choice either," I admitted. "But Mom promised me a trip to a gallery that was on my bucket list, in addition to vineyard tours, wine tastings, and yoga."

"Was it fun?" she asked.

"Yeah well, the yoga was fine," I said, "but Mom wasn't. Apparently she wanted to use the trip to have a 'talk' with me."

"A week-long talk?" Birdie asked incredulously. "She must've had a lot to say."

"She sure did. Apparently, I'm wasting my time here at Wellshire studying art," I said with more than a little bitterness. "Getting a 'silly art degree' is a waste of my time and her money, and if I wanted to paint, there was no reason I couldn't just 'play around' with it on the weekends."

She grimaced, knowing how this hit my pride. "Ouch."

"And it got better," I admitted. "She said while my degree might not be of any use, a husband sure would."

My stomach curdled at the words every time they played in my mind, and even more so when I actually spoke them out loud.

But when they'd come out of my mother's mouth? Well, that hurt. Like drive a dull dagger through my heart, kind of hurt.

I'd wanted to scream at her. I'd wanted to run. Instead, I just excused myself for the ladies' room, where I sat on the toilet seat with my head between my knees to ward off my nausea. I didn't know how to tell her what a vicious betrayal that sort of remark was. So, I didn't.

Birdie was equally indignant, sitting straight up and stomping her feet on the tile floor. "No *fucking* way!"

I nodded. "Yup. I mean, I wouldn't mind having a Steady Eddie. It would be fun. You know, someone to hang out with, have lots of sex with. Problem is, I've been back on campus for like, three hours now, and you know what? None of the guys around here do a damn thing for me. They're all… so lacking."

She looked at me knowingly. "Maybe, what you need isn't a student, but a *teacher*? Worked for me."

Before I could respond, there was a knock on my door. "Hey, bitches, open up!"

Roxy. My BFF had no filter sometimes, and as I opened the door, she exploded into the room like she always did. Although this time, she looked tired. She'd not had a nice little spring break vacation like Birdie and I had. No, Roxy's week off school meant nothing more than double shifts at her hotel maid job. My girl struggled to make ends meet, and worked herself to the bone every spare moment she had.

"So where's my weed?" I joked, a code phrase that Birdie and I came up with whenever we wanted save Roxy's feelings. When we used it, all conversation connected to money or our privilege stopped. I was pretty sure Roxy knew what we were doing, but she let it slide.

"Your weed is all smoked up, baby," Roxy said with a weak laugh.

Birdie nodded sagely. "Have a seat, we were just talking about Jessa's woes."

"Woes?" Roxy asked, and for the next few minutes I filled her in on what my mother had pressured me about, editing out the wine tastings and expensive shit.

"Well, we know what's on Mom's mind. She's not holding anything back," she said.

"Tell me about it," I sighed. "Neither of my parents takes me seriously. And I don't know if the art department does either. Like, my grades are fine, but I'm not getting the right doors opened."

"What would be the right door?" Roxy asked. "I mean, for the rest of the year?"

"That's easy," I said quickly. "I need to get into the Spring Show. It's for the best of the best of the undergrad art students, and if you're in, you get noticed. If I did well in that, I'd get a sweet scholarship. That'd let me cut the apron strings with the folks, and I'd get exposure to gallery owners. Last year's winner even got a summer-long residency at the Corning Museum in New York. A whole summer of all the mentoring you can handle, picking the minds of the artists in residence, making killer connections… yeah, it'd be sweet."

"That sounds amazing," Birdie said.

I sighed. "It would be. It truly would be. And looking back at the winners of the Spring Show, lots of them get offered residencies, internships, and fellowships that launched them upward. This goes for all sort of media, whether it's paint, metal, glass, or whatever. And supposedly you get matched to something that suits you. I mean, it'd be stupid to offer a fellowship at the Getty to someone who's more of a MoMA chick. Know what I mean?"

I saw that my two friends didn't, but they nodded along anyway. "So, you're right, Birdie. Oils are my thing, color on canvas." I tapped my fingers together. "Now... I just need to figure out how to get noticed."

2

GRIFF LEDGER

SOME OF THE department chairs at Wellshire University had professorial offices with oak bookshelves, antique desks, and the other bells and whistles you'd associate with being an academic of a certain standing.

Me? I had *space*. A space I loved. And it was exactly what I wanted, with good light, near floor to ceiling windows covering an entire wall, and a sizable area for my own painting projects. After all, when you're the chairman of the fine arts department, natural light is an imperative, nearly as vital as air to breathe. Fuck the fancy furniture. In one corner I had a saggy old velvet sofa someone was throwing out, perfect for afternoon naps and… other fun. In the other corner I had a rickety old bar cart I'd found at a flea market, which did a delightful job of holding my coffee maker and a couple bottles of my favorite spirits, squirreled away on the bottom shelf out of view of the department nosy bodies.

Hey, I was no prima donna. I didn't need an over-sized oak desk to feel like a big swinging dick the way some other academics did.

Although my job was not without its challenges. For one, I was the youngest chair at the school. Thirty four and running a department? It got me side-eyed looks at meetings, and even the occasional request for my student ID when I went to football games or other school events.

That, I didn't mind so much.

That afternoon I wasn't making art in my sunny office, though. It pained me, but I was doing the obligatory paperwork that sucked up my time on a regular basis. While being chair came with a good salary and the best working space in Wellshire, the detestable paperwork was almost endless. I had a good assistant, and he handled as much as he could. But there was some stuff that just demanded my attention.

So when there was a knock on my door, I was a little put out. I'd just gotten into the groove of doing my shit work, and now someone needed me?

"Yeah?" I barked.

The door opened, and a female voice asked, "Professor Ledger? Do you have a minute?"

Sighing, I got up and approached my door. Sure, I could have hollered for whomever it was to just come in, but I'd learned the hard way that once someone was all the way inside your office, it was much harder to get rid of them. If I met them at the door, on the other hand, and blocked their entrance—unless they really needed to come in—I could take care of business much faster and get back to work.

Yeah, I could be a dick that way. I just didn't have time to waste.

So when I yanked open my office door expecting one of my colleagues with a quick question, or a student griping about their grade, I was met with a pleasant surprise. If surprise was like saying the *Mona Lisa* was just a painting.

There stood one of my students. She was the sort of beauty born once a generation, maybe less. Her black hair gleamed in the light streaming through my windows, and her creamy skin flushed with the faintest pink over the apples of her cheeks. Her eyes were lined in the heavy fashion that seemed popular among certain girls at Wellshire, but instead of looking ridiculous, it was sexy as hell.

And that was just her face. Her body was another gift altogether from the heavens—tight, voluptuous... perfect.

We artists noticed stuff like this. It was our job.

"Hello. How can I help you?" I asked, trying not to stare like some kind of fucking creep.

"Professor Ledger... I'm Jessa Carr," she said, looking past me into my office, probably wondering why I wasn't inviting her in.

Believe me, I wanted to. While I had piles of stuff to do, I also wasn't sure I trusted myself.

"I took Basic Color Theory from you two semesters ago," she added hopefully.

No shit. I remembered. Honestly, how could I forget? Sitting on her stool in class, she looked like a muse herself, even if she wasn't trying to be overtly sexual. But a girl in fatigue pants and combat boots nearly always got my motor running.

Yeah, Jessa Carr just *was* sexy. More than that, she was a talented painter, with a good eye for color and decent technique. She'd been one of those students I'd noted, and had been tempted to take a more personal interest in her development.

So to speak.

But she was a young student, and off limits, at least with regard to any 'personal' sort of interest. So to save myself and my rep, I let her move on without any 'patronage.' The two semesters since then had just improved her beauty, giving it more maturity... and even more sexiness.

And her talent for oils had grown exponentially. I didn't think I'd ever seen anything quite like it.

"I remember you of course, Miss Carr," I said, stepping back to try and maintain some bearing. "What brings you by today? I don't normally have office hours on Mondays, especially since we just got back from spring break."

"I know, but... well, I'll just say it," she said, biting a soft, plump, luscious lip. She'd gone a bit goth that day, with lipstick a shade halfway between black and blood red, leaving me with thoughts of what that pretty mouth might do.

Professional, Griff. Remain professional.

"Really? What's up?" I asked.

"I *need* to get into the Spring Show," Jessa said quickly. "Seriously. Like, badly. What does it take?"

That was an easy question, if not one full of apprehension. "It takes good artwork, as I think you probably know. Now, if I remember right, you showed a lot of talent in your Color Theory class. Have you continued to improve?"

Like I hadn't followed her progress since day one. But she didn't need to know that.

"Well yes, I sure have," Jessa said, her pride chafed I'd even asked.

Which was good. An artist was supposed to have pride.

And she didn't stop at that. "I'm the best undergrad artist at Wellshire," she said, tilting her chin up a bit.

Damn. Confidence in spades. A woman who pulled no punches. I liked that.

"All right. Come on in and have a seat, Jessa," I said, gesturing toward one of the chairs in front of my paint-splattered desk.

Hell yes, this woman warranted an invite into my office.

"Let's look a little deep here. Getting into the Spring Show is a two-step process, as you know. First, you need a good piece."

"I've got that."

All righty then.

"Second," I continued, "is that you need an instructor to nominate you for the show. What art classes are you in this semester?"

Jessa listed off her schedule, and I saw the problem.

"Let me guess," I said as she finished. "You don't exactly suck up to your instructors, do you?"

"Well… is that a problem?" she asked.

I wanted to chuckle at her naivete. There she was, so beautiful, so sexy, so confident… and so utterly clueless about the dog-eat-dog reality of the art world. It was a very dangerous, and possibly very frustrating, combination for her.

"You see, the art world is a lot like many other career fields," I explained, hoping I didn't come off as a total douche. But she needed someone to tell her.

Confusion crossed her pretty face. I got it. I'd been there a long time ago. You think you can get by on the merit of your art, and when you find out that's not the case, well, it kind of fucks you up.

But I wasn't about to leave her out in the cold.

I continued. "Sometimes, it's not *what* you know, but *who* you know that gets you success. Now, you want to know about the most talented sculptor I've ever met?"

"Sure."

"His name was Gene Fordham, and I can already see you have no idea who he is. Neither does anyone else. You see, Gene Fordham wasn't famous. He never sold a piece for more than a hundred dollars in his lifetime. Gene was, in fact, a retired traffic cop who got into working with clay after his wife died. It was a sort of emotional therapy for him. Using just clay from his own backyard, kitchen tools, and some common paints, he could sculpt birds, trees, even people so life-like, so evocative, you'd swear he had taken the actual thing and encased it in a thin film of shellac."

"Okay," she said, clearly wondering why I was telling her this.

I shrugged, getting to the point of my tale. "Unfortunately for him, Gene Fordham was a grumpy, crusty old man who, when he wasn't making beautiful art, spent most of his time telling the neighborhood kids to get off his lawn. You get the picture. He never made business connections, never got a gallery show, and never got famous. The man was shitty at relationships, excuse my language. I found him, accidentally, when I was wandering around a flea market. He was selling his stuff out of the back of an old Suburban. Bought a piece of his for fifty dollars. It's at my house right now, displayed with art from other, very well-known sculptors. And it's just as good."

"Did you ever try and help him?" Jessa asked.

I chuckled. "When I offered him a business card, told him who I was, he promptly called me a 'hippie fairy' and tried to up the price on the piece I wanted."

Jessa winced. "Oh my god."

"So my point here, and I think you've probably figured it out, is that to get an invitation to the Spring Show, you've got to be more than good. You've got to have a sponsor. Some might call it a mentor, others a benefactor. All the great artists have had them. Da Vinci, Michelangelo, all of them. That means doing more than just art."

"Okay. Fine. I'll do *anything* to get into that show," she blurted.

Jesus, this woman was going to be the end of me.

And... below my belt was the familiar twitch, reminding me that while I might be a thirty-four year old man running a major department at a major university, my mammalian brain's top priority was still sticking my dick in things.

God help me.

Jessa caught herself before my dick totally ran away with my brain. "Um. You know what I mean," she said, tapering off in embarrassment.

Then she leaned forward, paint-stained fingers spread on my desk. "You see... well, I haven't told anyone else this. But my parents just threatened to cut off support for my schooling. They think I'm wasting my time studying art. I'm... devastated as you can imagine, not to mention, desperate. I don't know what I'm going to do," she said, her voice cracking on the last syllable. "That's why I'm bugging you about the Spring Show."

I'd heard that story once if I'd heard it a thousand times. Parents didn't want to spend their hard-earned money on art degrees for their children. They wanted their kids to study something 'respectable,' something that guaranteed them a good, steady living. Art was to be relegated to the 'hobby pile,' something people did in their free time if, once they had their nine-to-five job underway, they actually had any time left for.

Not something a serious person actually got a degree in.

But Jessa was clearly someone willing to fight that sentiment. She was looking for a way around it. Not giving in to the pressure of Mommy and Daddy.

I could get behind that.

I took a deep breath, reminding myself that I loved my job. That while I was a good artist, I was a better educator and developer of talent. And that Jessa Carr was a student.

And that meant… keep your distance, asshole.

"Okay, Jessa. You need to stand out more in the department. Get professors to notice you. Volunteer to help other students… maybe start tutoring. Cleaning up the art studios, or sticking around late to fire pottery. That kind of thing."

Jessa shifted in her seat, most likely uninterested in doing the shit work I was suggesting, but which would surely get her noticed. I didn't blame her. She was a college kid and probably relished every free moment she got.

In fact, if she were any other student, I'd have quickly ushered her out the door. You don't want to do the work? Then I can't help.

But I wasn't doing that to Jessa. No, I wanted her to stick around for a bit, at least until I convinced her of what she had to do to stand out.

Especially when she'd said she'd *do anything*.

"Professor, it's not that I don't want to help, but… is there another way?" she asked. "I mean, I suck at tutoring, and just ask my roommate about my cleaning skills."

That made me laugh. And, lucky for her, I did have one last idea. But I wasn't sure it was the kind of thing that would work for her. It was something of a long shot.

I took a deep breath. "Professor Dawson teaches a class called Life Drawing. Have you heard of it?"

"I think I have it next semester," she said, clearly wondering where I was going with this. "There's a live model that we draw every class, right?"

"Exactly, yes. There's a live model. And what I'm getting at is that they are short on models for this semester. It's easy work. You pose for fifty minutes, you get noticed… and you get paid."

Her face remained blank except for one eyebrow that arched up.

"Once you strike a pose, you have to be able to hold it until they tell you to change it. That can be a little challenging. Otherwise, it's a good gig."

If you didn't mind taking off your clothes in a room full of strangers.

"So… that'll help me get into the Spring Show?" she asked slowly.

Fuck me. She was interested.

I nodded. As much as I wanted to, I wasn't going to pressure her either way. She had to decide how badly she wanted to reach her goals. And I wasn't about to be the creep who pushed her into taking her clothes off. Much as I would have liked to.

Her eyes widened. "So, nude modeling. Like totally bare-ass naked?" she asked with a laugh.

I'd be dropping in on that class more than once, should she take the job.

"Bare-ass naked, as you put it. It's how students like you really understand how to draw the human body. You can't do portraiture without having practiced drawing nudes first."

She waved her hand dismissively. "Hell, I don't care about being naked. Not at all, especially if it will help me with the Spring Show. Besides, let's be honest, Professor. I'm at what's probably my physical prime. If I'm going to pose nude for anything, this is the time to do it. And the cash could be nice. It would give me at least some pocket money that I won't be getting from my folks."

I nodded, even if I didn't quite agree about there being a time limit on her looks. Jessa Carr had the kind of beauty that didn't fade, and her assumption that she'd already reached her peak was pretty absurd. She'd mature, just like we all did. Her perky breasts might be a little less so, and her heart-shaped bottom might get a little fleshier, but that face? Those eyes?

She was the kind of woman who'd be beautiful at fifty, sixty, and even longer.

I could see the hunger in her eyes. She wanted to be known for her talent, and be out from under the scrutiny of her parents. All for good reason.

"I'll tell you what, Jessa. I haven't used all of my nominations for the Spring Show. I'll propose a deal. You meet with Professor Dawson, and if he hires you for the job, that'll be half of what you need to get into the show."

"What's part two?"

Get on your knees, crawl over here, and swallow my... paintbrush.

God, I was an asshole.

"Bring me a piece worthy of the show," I told her, fighting my baser instincts. "Do that, and I'll make sure you get a spot. Winning it will be on you though. The judges aren't connected to the school in any way, so there's nothing anyone can do for you after that point."

"I'll take it," Jessa said, beaming as she popped to her feet. "Oh my god, thank you so much!"

She made a dash for the door, giving me a momentary view of the world's most perfect ass as it bounced inside her army pants

Her scent lingered, making it all the more difficult to gather my wits and get back to work. Oh to be a horny young undergrad guy again.

Well, I still had the horny part.

After struggling to get my head back into my paperwork, I bailed and headed home, where I found my colleague—and friend—the very Professor Dawson, chilling on my front porch, beer in hand.

"Griff, wassup, man?" he asked, pushing his messy hair back behind his ears.

He reached into the bucket of beers he'd set up next

to his chair, and retrieved a cold one. "Join me. Bought 'em this afternoon after class."

Using the hem of his faded concert T-shirt, he unscrewed the twist-off cap.

I took a long pull on the bottle. "Fantastic. Thank you. So, Indy, I have good news."

"You're not kicking me out, are you?" he joked.

We first met in college, two fine arts majors doing our best to blaze a trail in a crowded art world. I quickly realized that my talents didn't lie in making million dollar works of art, and turned to an academic life. But Indy stuck it out. Now, he was thirty four like me, and trying to dig himself out of a few financial holes after doing everything he could to get gallery representation.

Problem was, he'd come up empty, time and again, and not for any easily identifiable reason. His work was solid, and he was well-connected. He just hadn't been in the right place at the right time. Yet.

And while I relentlessly reminded him it was only a matter of time, my encouragement did not pay the bills. That's why, when a visiting professor slot opened up at Wellshire, I not only helped my friend out, but also let him crash in my spare bedroom. A semester later, he was still teaching and was now a certified housemate. We were a little crowded, especially since I had an in-law unit out back rented to another professor, Mason Acker, who spent a good deal of his free time with us guys in the main house.

But I wasn't complaining. I was probably having the

best time I'd had since I was a young guy in college, living with my buds.

I guess guys didn't grow out of everything.

Physically, Indy and I couldn't have been more different. I was clean cut, often wearing white button up shirts and tidy blue jeans. I figured as head of the department, it was the least I could do. I only stripped down when I was getting ready to paint.

But Indy was always ready to create art. His wardrobe consisted of holey jeans and faded T-shirts. If he was wearing clothing with no holes, well that was a cause for celebration. In fact, I'd gone out and bought him new T-shirts after three students complained that it was hard to focus in class when the tongue of his Rolling Stones t-shirt looked like it was licking his nipple.

Add to that the scraggly hair he was perpetually tucking behind his ears, the wire-rimmed glasses that always sat a little askew due to a broken nose in childhood, and Indy Dawson was… well, pretty much your standard artist. Funky, eccentric, weird… and a damn good friend.

"You're not being kicked out yet. I'm saving that for next week," I teased. "Actually, I did you a solid this afternoon. Found you another model for your Life Drawing class. You did say you were looking for someone, right?"

I expected a grin, or maybe a thank you. Instead, he groaned. "Fuuuuck, Griff. A new model, halfway through the semester? Please tell me he's not as bad as the last one."

"What was wrong with the last one?" I asked. "You never quite told me the details, just said the guy flaked out after two sessions."

"Didn't want to embarrass the kid, so I kept my mouth shut," he admitted. "Look, it happens sometimes, but that guy was rock fucking hard about fifteen seconds after taking off his robe. Again, it happens, but that little cockhound stayed hard the whole goddamn class. He was literally dripping precum by the end of fifty minutes."

I burst out laughing so hard I nearly spat my beer. "No fucking way. I did not know that."

I could just imagine the little perv getting turned on, freaking out all the girls in class. And undoubtedly some guys, as well.

Indy laughed too. "Kid was obviously an exhibition-ist, and I'm not trying to throw shade. But first off, it disrupted class. People were whispering and giggling the whole time, which I think just turned him on more. Second, it wasn't like he had a lot to be proud of, if you know what I mean. So yeah, I had to let him go."

"Well, that won't be a problem this time."

He looked at me skeptically. "You sure? Griff, let's be honest. Live models are ninety percent of the time weirdos. Like, remember when we were undergrads?"

I laughed at the memory. "Mr. Starfish?" I asked, and he nodded.

"How that sick fuck was able to hold his ass cheeks

apart for a whole class session without cramping is something I still haven't figured out," he said with a laugh. "Although it made for a good drawing."

I groaned. "I remember turning in my charcoal and ink drawing of that puckered sphincter, and promptly burning those pens and pencils. Wish I could burn the image of his asshole from my brain."

"So seriously, what's up with this one, this new model you swear is what I need?" he asked, still not convinced I wasn't sending some weirdo his way.

"Nothing's wrong with *her*," I said.

In fact, she was so perfect I hated to share her. But I also wanted to help her, so I put my greediness aside.

"Her name's Jessa Carr, and she's… well, I'll let you see for yourself. You won't be disappointed."

"*She?*" Indy asked, lifting an eyebrow. "*Really?*"

I nodded. "Yup. One look, and you're going to love her. Just remember—"

"Don't love her too much," he finished for me.

3

JESSA CARR

"HOW WAS your visit with Professor Delicious?"

The dining hall was in full-on pandemonium, with people rushing to get a bite to eat in between classes. So, it was a massive relief that Birdie, Roxy, and I decided to take our lunch outside.

Birdie grinned at me around a mouthful of ham sandwich. I was dying to ask how she was able to eat so much and not gain any weight... but I had a strong suspicion about how she was burning off any extra calories.

I knew she'd be grilling me about my meeting. Hell, I would have done the same to her. She knew how important this was to me

"His name is Professor Ledger, and it was fine," I said primly.

But even Roxy rolled her eyes.

She looked between Birdie and me. "What? What's going on? What did I miss?"

"Come on, Jessa," Birdie said. "We know your department head looks like a buff Ryan Reynolds, and not the *Deadpool* one either. You can't tell us that a little bit of you didn't enjoy going to his office."

Roxy sighed. "Oh. *That* professor. Seriously. I wish I had a hot professor to visit."

"You *do*, Roxy," I protested. She started to smile, but then covered her teeth, clamping her lips together. I knew why, but didn't want to press the point. "Anyway, it went well. He gave me some good guidance, and even made me a deal. I help out around the department, bring him a show-worthy piece, and I'll get my spot in the spring show."

Even saying the words made me want to jump up and down. I was as good as in. I knew not to count my chickens, but it was hard not to.

"Really?" Birdie said with a lascivious grin. "You *help out*, and you'll get a slot?"

I rolled my eyes at her air quotes. "It's not like that, Bird."

She shook her head, unconvinced. "Yeah, but Griff Ledger's hot... and if he says his department needs help, well, you'd better step up to the plate, girlie."

"You're so lucky, Jess. I'm jealous," Roxy added. "I mean, you all know *my* department chair, Professor Handley."

I shivered, knowing what she meant. Nathaniel Handley was perhaps one of the strangest-looking men I'd ever seen. In his seventies, he should have retired years before. Tufts of rough white hair erupted from his ears and nose, and he was infamous for cracking his hairy knuckles as he taught, like little firecrackers going off at the oddest times.

"Hey, if we should be jealous of anyone, shouldn't it be Birdie here?" I pointed out. "I mean, she's got three hot profs to help with all her needs—academic, physical, emotional. You name it."

Birdie just stretched her legs out, catching some sun and looking happy. "You could too. Both of you could have what I do. I mean, you're hot enough to get the attention, obviously. By the way, Jess, what'll you be doing to help out?"

"Modeling for Life Drawing," I replied, a little too quickly. "I get paid for it, too. Not much, I'm sure, but it's better than helping out for free."

"Wait... Life Drawing?" Roxy said, biting the tip of her tongue as she thought. "I've heard of that course. Isn't that where they have a nude model and the students draw them? Like for an entire semester? You're going to do that? In front of other students?"

"Yeah. So?" I asked.

But before Birdie or Roxy could comment, my phone rang.

"Hold on... it's my mom."

Leaving Birdie and Roxy to marvel that I was going to be dropping trou in a classroom of artists, I ran over to a nearby bench for some privacy. "Hey, Mom, what's up?"

"What's up?" Mom asked, sighing. "All sorts of things are *up*, Jessa. After the good time we had together on spring break, I talked with your father. We're going to do it."

"Do *what?*"

The next spring break was a year off, leaving me plenty of time to let my mother know we'd not be repeating this year's trip. I wasn't getting into a conversation about it this far in advance, though. But our mother-daughter trips were over.

Mom laughed in amusement. "Why, we're coming for parents' weekend, silly. After all you told me about it, I couldn't let you down. I can't wait to see the Wellshire campus again… and meet the special guy in your life."

Somewhere in the background, karma laughed its fucking ass off at me. And my stomach flipped multiple times, killing my interested in lunch.

That's what I got for bringing up parents' weekend. Mom and Dad had not been interested in attending in previous years, so I never thought they'd bother this time.

Which had left me free to make up a big story about a fake-ass boyfriend. As in, a boyfriend I didn't have.

"Honey? Are you still there?" Mom asked.

I blinked, realizing I'd gone into a near catatonic state. "Ugh, yeah, Mom. Yeah, that's great… Hey, I don't want to cut you short, but I need to wrap this up. I've got a meeting with a professor."

"No problem, honey," she said. "I'll e-mail you tonight and we can work out the details. See you soon!"

The line went dead, a lot like my spirits, and I

zombie-walked back to Roxy and Birdie, who were giggling together until they saw my dire expression.

"What happened?" Roxy asked, alarmed. "You look like somebody died."

I plopped to the ground, not trusting myself to remain standing. "Remember how I told you on Sunday that Mom was giving me the talk about getting my M-R-S degree?"

"Oh god. More of that?" Roxy asked.

If only I'd kept my big damn mouth shut.

"Well…. it gets worse. See, I didn't tell you everything. To get Mom off my ass, I sort of… made up a boyfriend."

Birdie started to snicker, then clamped a hand over her mouth and stopped. She knew I wasn't in the mood.

"You… made up… a boyfriend?" Roxy asked. "Holy shit. Are you crazy?"

"I needed Mom off my back!" I snapped. "She was dropping hints, then just got super direct, saying that if I didn't get serious about 'doing what I needed to in college,' she and dad would cut me off."

"The *fuck?!?*" Roxy exclaimed. Considering how much she was struggling to make ends meet, she was very sensitive to money issues of any kind. "Whatever the hell for?"

"Because they see art as being a bullshit degree," Birdie said for me.

I'd been about to say the words. But they'd gotten stuck in my throat.

I wasn't going to cry. I wasn't going to freak out. I was keeping my shit together.

I steadied my voice. "You know how it is. A lot of degrees, you can get scholarships for. Art, not so much. Unless I end up being one of the Spring Show winners."

"So you've got to go win that fucker then," Roxy said. "That's all there is to it. Seriously, babe. You've got the talent. Go fucking get it."

But there was that pesky, shorter term problem. "Yeah but... in the meantime, they're coming up for parents' weekend. If I don't want a shit show, I've gotta find something to distract them. And I've got to come up with a guy."

Shit, shit, shit. I'd heard Mom's hints about pulling the plug on me. I just didn't think they'd do it this soon.

Would they even let me finish the school year?

"I'd lend you a man, but no way would your parents think the guys were students," Birdie said. "I mean, they'd do it to help you, but your cover would get blown in about thirty seconds."

I wouldn't mind borrowing one of Birdie's men. For any reason.

"Thanks Birdie, really. I appreciate that," I said, knowing she was a hundred percent serious, and a hundred percent right that it would never fly. "So what do I do?"

"Just find a guy for the weekend," Birdie said. "Seriously, Jessa. You've got a fan club bigger than Taylor

Swift's here on campus. Just pick a decent looking guy, play it up for the weekend, then drop him."

Roxy looked at her phone when it beeped, signaling time to get to work. "Darn, I gotta bounce. I don't want to, but I have to get my shift in. Birdie, you mind if I use your bed tonight? I'd rather crash here on campus than at my parents'. Things are… tense there."

Before Birdie could even answer, I grabbed Roxy's hand and squeezed it. "Oh my god, yes!" I was thrilled to have Roxy crash in Birdie's empty bed. I needed the company.

Birdie handed Roxy her key. "It's all good, babe. I'll be working at the library until it closes, then… well, you know. Unless you need me to stay around, Jessa?"

I shook my head, waving her off. "Roxy, remember to bring some cookies?"

She grinned and flashed me a tired thumbs up. "Will do."

Roxy took off, and out of the corner of my eye I spotted someone I knew. He was just another Wellshire student I'd seen around, whom I was pretty sure lived in a dorm near mine. I might not even have noticed him just then if he hadn't been working in the cafeteria that day. In fact, he'd bagged up my lunch.

He was reasonably handsome, polite, and… bland. Someone I could possibly recruit to be at my side long enough for parents' weekend, and then walk away from without any major issues.

"Birdie, you know what?" I said, climbing to my

feet. "You may have just given me an idea. I'll check in with you at the library later."

"The library?" Birdie asked, also getting to her feet. "What the hell do you need that place for, unless you want to use the stacks on the reference floor? They're quite popular with people having clandestine sex. I saw, or should I say *heard*, a couple going at it just yesterday when I was reshelving books."

I wanted to ask if she'd messed around with any of the professors there, but I didn't have time.

I had to save my college career.

4

INDY DAWSON

"See you Thursday, Professor Dawson!" A student of mine, a blonde with a streak of pink in her hair, gathered her paints and other tools into her monogrammed tote bag. She was a terrible painter, and had almost no sense of flow or balance. But she was taking Intro to Art, one of the classes around Wellshire that was often used by students to just get an easy elective credit.

Besides, in a class where half the grade depended on 'peer evaluations,' this student was going to easily skate through on her popularity. I had suspicions about just how she was able to so consistently get top marks from her peers, based off of her reputation. But I wasn't going to raise a fuss. It was an elective, not for serious artists.

I had no illusion that I was teaching a classroom of Picassos.

Once everyone had cleared out, I started on my own class notes. I preferred to work in the classroom rather than my office, the tiny, stuffy space that somehow fit three desks in a Jenga-Tetris-like fashion. I shared it with two other associate professors, but honestly preferred to do as much of my work as possible in one of the art studios. There, I could spread out, enjoy the natural light, and breathe the scent of paints.

Which I found oddly appealing.

Before I could get much further than putting my pen to paper, the classroom door opened, and I looked up to see a vision walk through. Glossy black hair, a sexy body that perfectly walked the line between athletic and voluptuous, combat boots to go along with her short skirt... I knew who it was even before she opened her mouth.

"Professor Dawson? I'm Jessa Carr. Professor Ledger told me to come talk with you. We have an appointment, right?"

I looked down, checking my watch. It was three forty-two in the afternoon. She was right, I'd gotten an e-mail from Griff that morning telling me about the appointment he'd set up with the potential life drawing model he'd been so excited about. I'd just not taken it very seriously. After all, Jessa Carr was an art student. Artists are many things... punctual and reliable aren't usually one of them.

But not only had she arrived three minutes early, she'd found me in my classroom rather than my office.

Resourceful.

I pushed my paperwork aside. "First, call me Indy. Second, I'm impressed to see you here."

I might have been wearing a Run DMC T-shirt and old black jeans, but I did hold myself to certain levels of professionalism. And Jessa Carr just lifted herself up in my eyes. She was worthy of my full attention.

"Are you *sure* you're an art student?"

"Huh?" Jessa asked, tilting her head and looking… fucking sexy. God, those lips. "What do you mean?"

"I mean you're the first appointment I've had all week that showed up on time," I told her honestly. "Artists tend to be the flakiest people around. Including myself."

Jessa laughed, a sexy sound that could easily inspire an artist to works worthy of the great masters. But instead, I forced myself to remain professional and to focus, in spite of myself. I wasn't sure whether I loved or hated Griff for sending her my way. I'd have to decide that later.

She nodded, swingy hair bouncing around her face. "I understand. My best friend and my roommate are both punctual types. I guess it's rubbed off on me. So… I hear you need a live model?"

"We sure do. The last one was… well, never mind," I said, chuckling.

I tried not to obviously look her up and down, but it was near impossible. Her black tank-top clung to her curves, and her short skirt showed a ton of leg from mid-thigh to the tops of her combat boots. She even had knee high socks on.

Damn, she was all sorts of goth-rock princess, a dash of punk and pretty much everything my dick liked. Even her smile was sexy.

"Well, I just want to be sure you know I'm an artist. Modeling is just to… you know, um, make a little money," she declared. "But I still would like the job."

"Well first, let's discuss the details. The pay is twenty five dollars per session. I know that's not a lot, but it's all the department budgets for models."

She nodded, clearly doing the math in her head. Twenty five dollars for less than an hour's work? That was hard to beat for any college student.

"Sounds great. How many sessions a week would you need me?"

I thought for a moment. "Depending on your availability, there's a drawing class almost every day, sometimes two. But that wouldn't guarantee you'd get it. There are other students who pose, and I insist that students learn to draw all types of physiques."

"I get that. I mean, imagine if all artists could only draw Botticelli-esque asses?" She laughed.

Oh trust me, Sandro Botticelli would have killed to paint you.

"Speaking of Botticelli and his style," I said, "You are aware you're going to need to hold a pose for as long as an hour sometimes? And that you'll be required to be nude?"

"Sure," she said, nodding calmly. "Something like this?"

Before I could react, she pushed her skirt down and

pulled off her tank top. Underneath she was wearing a nearly invisible black lace thong and bra that left nothing to the imagination. I could clearly see her tight, eraser shaped nipples and the crinkly pale areola surrounding them, her tight, flat stomach, and the light tan lines framing a shaved pussy that looked so soft... well shit, I grabbed a table for balance.

She half turned, putting her arms out in front of her like she was pushing off an invisible ballet barre, arching her back just enough to emphasize the gorgeous curve and peach of her ass. She froze, showing me her ability to pose. Just like that. No shit.

I stared for a long ten seconds, my eyes drinking in the figure of feminine perfection in front of me. Somehow, her keeping her boots on made her pose even sexier, and in my mind I could imagine them pressed against my chest as I drove my cock into her willing, supple body.

A sound came from the hallway, and I blinked, suddenly aware that I was in a classroom, alone, with a ridiculously beautiful undergrad who was wearing about one ounce of transparent clothing. I opened my mouth to say something, but my throat was suddenly dry, and all the blood in my brain was on a one way trip to my crotch.

I cleared my throat, hoping to find my voice. "What are you doing, Miss Carr?"

She gave me a curious look. "Trying out, of course."

I let out a long breath, almost laughing in relief and maybe a little disappointment that she wasn't posing for me just because she wanted to. "Yeah, well um, there's no try-out process. Now let's get you a robe."

"Oh thanks, but not necessary," she said, relaxing her body and standing with one hand on her hip. Completely unselfconscious.

She bent for her skirt and as she did, she unintentionally gave my balls another jolt as she exposed the sweet slit of her pussy. Once her skirt was back in place, she bent again for her top, pulling it over her head before tucking it in.

Now that she was clothed, I could at least think semi-clearly again. "First off, you're hired for the job. But I have a recommendation."

"What's that?" she asked, her smile spreading across her face. "Oh, it doesn't matter, I'm just so grateful for the job! I promise I'll be everything you need."

She had to realize what she was doing, right? But I remained professional, much as I didn't want to.

"You're welcome," I said, steadying my voice. "But what I wanted to say was, I suggest choosing simple, relaxed poses unless you've got legitimate experience. Fifty minutes of what you just did would be awfully hard to hold."

She grinned and shrugged. "Don't worry, Professor. I do yoga, and when I was little, my parents had me in ballet class. That's where the pose came from, really."

I could just imagine her other 'poses.'

She slung her bag over her shoulder. "Anyway, when do I start?"

Reminded of my professional duties again, I opened

the department's shared calendar on my phone. "How about… next Thursday at three? And again, please call me Indy."

"Can do, Profess—I mean, Indy," she said eagerly. "And… thank you again."

After she left and my erection had gone down enough to no longer be painful, strangled as it had been by my blue jeans, I checked the calendar again. The truth was, there were more open sessions. Several. I wasn't the only instructor teaching Life Drawing, and we could use all the models we could get. But suddenly, I didn't want to share her.

I wanted that beauty all to myself.

It was a dick move, I know.

But Griff had said she might need the money. I gave myself a reminder to talk to her about other classes. If she needed the work, I wouldn't stand in her way.

I got the rest of my paperwork done and headed home. Of course, it wasn't *my* home, since I shared it with Griff. But it felt that way, even if it was just temporary. When Griff got me the position at Wellshire, he said he'd help me either get the school to pay for a place, or help me find an apartment, but he ended up putting me up himself. Not that he didn't like my staying with him, but it occasionally put a crimp on our social lives. He already had another tenant in the 'in-law quarters' out back—a Comms professor named Mason Acker.

Mason was a good guy whom I'd come to consider a friend. Still, there were issues having three single guys at the same address. Neckties on doorknobs stopped being acceptable once we'd left our undergrad days behind.

Once home, I changed clothes for a quick workout, climbed on the Stairmaster Griff kept in his basement, and started mindlessly climbing to try and distract myself from thoughts of Jessa Carr. I was about three quarters done when I heard the door upstairs open, and Griff's footsteps.

"Indy?" he called.

"Yeah man, got another five minutes," I yelled back. "What's up?"

Griff came downstairs, untucking his clean white shirt from his jeans. "Hey. Just wanted to see if Jessa Carr came to that appointment you had."

"Oh yeah," I said, and Griff gave me a second look.

"What do you mean, *oh yeah*? Was she able to get the job?"

I glanced at the Stairmaster, and figured fuck it, I could skip the last few minutes. "Hold on. Grab some beers and we can talk in the kitchen."

Griff went upstairs while I slowed and then stopped. Using my T-shirt as a towel, I wiped down my upper body before wrapping it around my shoulders. I walked upstairs and sat at the kitchen island, where Griff already had a Corona open for me.

"Thanks," I said, taking a deep pull. The cool beer probably wasn't the best post-workout drink, but it certainly helped steady my nerves. "Now, as for Jessa Carr… yes, she came by the classroom. Early in fact."

"Very good," Griff said, drumming his fingers. Obviously, he'd been nervous over the whole thing. "And how did it go?"

"Well, let's see," I said, running my finger over the rim of the bottle. "You remember back to our under-grad days, the class we took on the history of human photography?"

"Ah," Griff said, nodding. "I think I see where you're going. She does look a lot like a classic pinup model, Bettie Page or Dita Von Teese, but—"

"She got naked," I said, and Griff's face fell like I'd thrown a switch. "I mean, not totally naked, she was wearing this sheer bra and thong set that left nothing to the imagination, but…"

My mind went back to the image of Jessa posing for me, one leg cocked slightly back, her hair thrown over her shoulders to cascade down her back, the three quarters curve of one perfect breast visible from my angle. It was seared into my memory, the way her eyes were half lidded, her lips succulent and suckable, and—

"Indy? Indy!" Griff said, and I realized that one, I'd been daydreaming, and two, I was hard as a rock in the cutoff sweatpants I used for exercise shorts. "She… stripped for you?" he asked skeptically.

Griff said it in such a way I could tell he was seeing her in his mind too, and was probably mad as hell it hadn't been he who'd gotten the show.

"Yeah," I finally managed, taking another drink. "I signed her up for a spot next Thursday. I mean, art students who can keep to schedule are rare."

Griff, who knew a thing or two about that, laughed. "Hey, those are our students you're talking about!"

I shrugged, tipping my bottle at him. "Look who's talking? I'm not the one who missed the last bus back to campus from that museum field trip we took."

"There was a good reason for that!" Griff protested with bitter laughter. "Two of them, in fact, if I remember right. And you thanked me when she 'reasoned' all over you the following weekend."

There was one certain, totally uncontroversial truth about our friends from the museum all those years ago.

Jessa Carr made them, even combined, look like a couple of bag ladies.

5

JESSA CARR

"When are your Mom and Dad coming?"

Shit. Had I made a terrible mistake by asking Cole to be my pretend 'boyfriend' for parents' weekend? The truth was, even though I'd tried to be very, very clear with him that this was all a sham, a smokescreen in order to get my parents off my back, he seemed to be taking it a little more seriously than he should. Like, way too seriously. As if he thought it was the real thing. Twice I'd found him waiting for me outside class, ready to walk me to my next one.

Yeah, fake boyfriends don't do that.

If I hadn't been so desperate, I would have paid more attention to the warning bells sounding in my desperate brain, of which there were many. I hadn't even told him my class schedule, but there he was, like a damn stalker. But all I could think about at the time was that Cole was just the sort of guy I knew my parents would like. Clean-cut but not too nerdy, he was the sort of preppy but well behaved frat boy that my father swore he was in his college days, the kind that 'have a plan,' and 'go places in life.'

And, my mother would add, the sort of nice young man one might meet at the *club*. If I ever went to the club. Which I did not. I hated the club. The last time I'd been there was for a friend's Bat Mitzvah, back in middle school.

So, as eager as Cole seemed to be my *real* boyfriend, ours was a great temporary arrangement and I was sticking with it. I really had no other choice. I reminded myself he was doing me a solid, and to be grateful for his help. His crush on me was cute and harmless. He was the Golden Retriever of guys.

At least I thought so.

"They'll be here any minute," I said nervously, checking my phone for the inevitable 'we're here!' text message from Mom. "Remember, they'll be around for just today. So let's go over the plan."

"Okay, okay," he said easily, leaning against the wall in my dorm room. Since he was my 'boyfriend,' I'd invited him in to talk plans, but with the very clear rule that he was to stay in the entrance area only. No sitting on beds or even getting near the beds.

He repeated what I'd already had him say several times. "You're going to go down, meet the folks and give them the campus tour. When that's over, you'll text me and we'll meet up for introductions."

"Perfect. And how long have we been dating?" I

asked, switching into quiz mode. "Where was our first date?"

"It was the football game against State, and we went because you felt sorry for me after tripping me in the dining hall and making me sprain my wrist." He rolled his right hand around with a fake wince. "After the game, you realized that football wasn't all that bad, in limited doses, and since then it's been a sort of opposites attract thing."

Okay. Good. We'd worked on a few more details, nothing too crazy, but I needed to make sure all was in order. "And after that?"

"We'll go out for a family dinner, some place casual but not too casual. I'll offer to pay, but your father will insist on covering the bill. After that, we'll say goodbye to your parents, and that'll be that."

There was so much as stake for me that I wanted more reassurance, but before I could ask for it, my phone buzzed. "Okay. That's Mom. I figure in an hour, maybe two, you'll hear from me. I'll text you and we'll start."

"Cool, I'll be waiting… *snookums*," he said with a smirk.

"Oh *hell* no," I told him. "And no babe, sugar, or any of that. Keep it to Jess, please."

I left the dorm and hurried down to the campus visitor parking lot, where I found Mom and Dad parking their new BMW. That was Dad, a big believer in looking the part. And as an upper-mid-level executive for a home finance company, that meant driving a Beamer.

"Jessa, honey!" Dad called, hugging me before stepping back and giving me a look. "I see that you're still on this… fashion thing."

An insincere smile flashed across his face and he turned his attention to the noisy jet passing overhead.

"Oh hush, Ronald, all the kids do it," Mom said, coming around to give me a hug too. "Besides, she's just copying our generation. Or don't you remember the goth and grunge trends?"

"I remember… but I wish it had stayed in the past where it belongs." He looked around, nodding. "It's still a pretty campus."

"Dad, they didn't just uproot the entire university since the last time you were here," I pointed out, trying to stay positive. I needed them on board with me. "Come on, let's take a walk."

"When are we going to meet your boyfriend?" Mom asked.

Guess we knew her priorities.

I cleared my throat, forcing a smile. "Later, Mom. He's got a job in the cafeteria and can't meet up until his shift's over."

"Good man, putting business first," Dad said. "Well, lead on, Jessa."

For the next hour and a half, I led my parents around the art department buildings, showing them the various classrooms and studios where my classmates and I created art. Not that they were particularly interested. Unfortunately.

"It's... a vase," Dad said as I showed them the pottery room. There was actually one of my pieces in there, which I did the prior semester. While I knew I was never going to be a ceramicist, it did sting to see my father dismiss my hours of hard work as just 'a vase.'

"Well, ceramics isn't my forte," I told them, "but I'm working on a piece now that I am really proud of."

"A painting?" Mom asked, and I nodded. "That's nice," she said blandly.

I gritted my teeth and continued. I could tell with every shallow comment or tolerant glance between them that they thought I was wasting my time at Wellshire, not that it was a secret they felt that way. But to see it up close and in person, well that brought disappointing to a new level. Finally, I couldn't stand it any longer and pulled out my phone, texting Cole.

"Great news," I told my parents, "he's off work and will meet us outside my dorm."

"Oh that's wonderful!" Dad said, clearly glad to be done with my art tour.

Time for the main event, at least as my parents saw it. That was made even clearer when they saw Cole. There was none of the wariness, none of the 'so what are you doing with my daughter' sort of questions that most parents have for a new boyfriend.

No, with my parents. Their seeing Cole was like the

giddiness of showing a little girl her new Christmas pony.

"It's so nice to meet you. You're so clean cut!" my mother gushed, like she couldn't believe the 'boyfriend' I'd spoken of was a walking, talking, decent human being.

Cole, getting into character, draped an arm around my shoulder and laughed. "I know, I'm a little country, and Jessa's a little thrash death metal. But it works."

All right, Cole. Damn. He knew how to play my parents like a fiddle. Not that he had to try too hard. They were ripe for any sort of half-alive male I might bring around. Seeing him with his arm around my shoulder, or holding my hand as he was now, they were practically eating out of his palm.

"So what are you studying?" Dad asked as we walked past the football stadium, right after Cole told Dad our 'first date' story.

I was psyched. This guy was laying it on and my parents couldn't be happier.

"Computer engineering," he said, grinning. "It's a good career path that has near unlimited growth potential and a secure job market."

Tick, tick, tick, tick... I could practically see my father marking up his mental checklist, and Cole was hitting them all. Mom, of course, had slightly different concerns.

"What about family?" Mom asked.

"Mom!"

Cole laughed. "That's a bit fast, Mrs. Carr, but I'll

tell you. I'm an only child, and to be honest, it sort of sucked growing up that way. I'd like to have a large family, as long as we can support them."

If we'd lived in another country, one where selling your daughter was still legal, I'd have been sold right there. Just bring the receipt by later. Hell, they probably would have freaking given me away, that's how much they liked Cole.

That's how done my parents were. They were Team Cole, hook, line, and sinker.

Dinner was as expected, at a chain steakhouse near campus that was nice enough, serving stuffed mushrooms with our steaks.

"Mr. Carr, Mrs. Carr, I just wanted to say thank you," Cole said.

While he'd held my hand and put his arm around me, he hadn't pressed for anything else. In fact he'd been rather charming, and part of me wondered for a fraction of a second why I'd sworn off college guys.

Get a grip.

"Thank us for what, Cole?" Dad said, sipping at his beer. He was letting himself have one, and only one, with dinner. He liked being under control like that.

"For raising such a beautiful daughter."

Oh god. I had to bite my tongue not to laugh.

Cole turned to give me a warm look. "She's such a beautiful soul, I know at least some of it had to come from you."

Okay, that was enough. I kicked him under the table to stop. I didn't want to lose my dinner.

In spite of Cole laying it on, everything was a cake-walk after that. Mom and Dad were thrilled I'd finally 'met someone,' and Cole was even able to help when Mom or Dad would toss a little shade at my art studies.

As we walked out, Mom whispered in my ear, "Hang onto this one, honey. He's a keeper."

I nodded, not saying anything, but I could see Cole smirk a little up ahead of us. He'd heard.

In the parking lot, I exchanged hugs with Mom and Dad, while Cole shook hands with Dad before giving Mom a friendly hug. I watched them get in Dad's Beamer, pulling away for the two hour drive back home.

"Well now, that went well, didn't it?" Cole said as we started walking back toward the dorms. "They liked me."

"They did. You did a great job," I told him. "Thanks so much. I really appreciate it."

"Thanks?" he said, giving me a strange look. "That's all I get?"

"Come on, Cole," I said, little alarm bells going off. "You got a good dinner, and I already promised you a hundred bucks. Just give me a week or two to get it, that's all."

"I think I deserve more than that," he said, grabbing my arm and pulling me to him. He was fast, almost too fast, and I barely was able to turn my face as he tried to kiss me.

"Cole!"

"Come on, baby," he growled, trying to grope my ass

as he refused to let go. "Hell, your own momma said don't let this one get away."

What had happened to the polite, mild-manner computer student I'd just spent the evening with?

"I… no!" I yelled, pushing him as hard as I could. It didn't break his grip, but my combat boot smashing down on his loafer certainly did. I pushed again, backing away as fast as I could. "No!"

"You… you cock tease me all week," he hissed, limping slightly as he walked after me, "and all I get is a cheap ass steak?"

I didn't want to run, worried that even with a stomped foot Cole could catch me. He was at least five inches taller, and most of my workouts weren't the running kind. I'd never been a superstar sprinter, even when I wasn't wearing combat boots.

Just as he'd caught up with me and grabbed my arm, a guardian angel arrived. "Hey! Get the fuck away from her!" a deep voice boomed through the parking lot.

Cole froze, and heavy footsteps hurried our way. But before I could see who they belonged to, my 'date' took off, half limping as he did.

"Are you okay?" the man asked, approaching.

I turned, shocked when I saw who it was. "Professor Acker… you saved me."

I was part relieved, and part humiliated to have one of my professors find me in such a shitty situation. Mason Acker taught Introduction to Public Communications, my elective for the semester after Birdie suggested I could use the skills in the class to assist with pitching my art. In class, Acker always looked sort of like a lawyer or a politician, with expertly gelled hair and piercing blue eyes, a strong jawline, and even a dimple on his chin. Still, he wasn't intimidating… until that night.

"*Jessa*," he said, immediately identifying me. "What happened? What the hell was that?"

"Just… a miscommunication with a friend," I answered, shivering.

The shakes got stronger, and I knew in my head what it was. Adrenaline was surging now, my body forced into flight or fight mode. The fear and anger resulting from Cole's confrontation was pulsing its way through my nerves… I knew all that, but it didn't stop my body shakes, or its intensity.

Carefully, Professor Acker wrapped an arm around my shoulders. "I don't like what I just saw. Not at all."

I leaned into him and felt so overwhelmingly safe. Thank goodness he'd happened by.

"You want me to call the cops, Jessa?"

I shook my head. "If he talks to me again, I'm putting a combat boot in his nuts."

Acker hummed. "Just be careful. I enjoy you in my class too much to see you hurt."

I knew his words were just being nice, but as he pulled me tighter, an instinctual need swept through me. Looking up at him, I saw those blue eyes, his sensuous mouth, the concern in his face, and I couldn't stop myself. Standing on my tiptoes, I kissed him. I couldn't explain why. It was almost like a reflex, with no conscious thought involved.

For a moment, he kissed me back. But then he stopped, almost regretfully if I was reading him correctly. "Thank you, but there's no need for that, Jessa. Are you sure you're safe?"

What the fuck had I done that for? God, I was an idiot, and now I had to see this man in class. Jesus.

"I am fine, thank you again, Professor Acker. Sorry. I shouldn't have done that." I brought my hand to my forehead to make sure all my brains hadn't magically leaked out or something.

"Mason. Call me Mason," he said. "And let's just forget it ever happened."

I hoped he'd forget, but me? I wouldn't be forgetting anytime soon.

His lips were so soft and he smelled so damn good…

Down girl.

"I'll see you Monday, then," he said.

But before I could lose my nerve, I darted in and kissed him again, and again for a second, he kissed me back, his hands coming to my waist before I pulled away this time. I walked off, my boots clicking on the pavement.

I'd just kissed a professor. One of *my* professors.

A very handsome, sexy professor.

After spending an entire day pretending to have a boyfriend.

Was I losing my damn mind?

6

MASON ACKER

"Yo, Mason!"

My old Honda clattered as I pulled into the driveway of Griff's house and shut it off. I barely heard it, still sort of numb and in shock from the unexpected kiss I'd just gotten from a student.

Indy greeted me from the porch as I got out. Living with two other guys was turning out to be a better set-up than I'd expected. While I'd initially hesitated because I didn't want anyone in my business, it turned out the guys I shared with were more than respectful, and actually a lot of fun.

I hadn't realized how much I missed living with friends.

That might sound kind of juvenile for a thirty-something dude like me, but what can I say? We guys drank beers together, watched games, and talked endlessly about the ups and downs of academic life. And there were a lot of those.

Indy's gripe was that he wasn't a 'real' professor. Despite his repeated efforts at becoming a commercially successful artist, and a semester and a half of good teaching where he showed a flair for communicating with his students, he swore he was taking the academic route only temporarily until he could get some gallery or another to run another show for him. I felt for him. I knew what it was like to want something so badly you could taste it.

Meanwhile, Griff was busy trying to get respect for a department that was constantly in danger of getting its funding cut. In an era where government officials and alumni were all about budget, fine arts was in even more danger than music, film, or archeology.

At least, as part of the English department, I was seen as a more or less necessary evil. People had to be able to communicate, and every last college student had to take at least a couple English classes. Talk about guaranteed employment. And the administration liked my idea of combining English and public speaking, something the school had never had before, even if I did hear one douchebag alum call it 'PowerPoint 101.'

All of that was just background noise as I climbed the wooden steps to the porch, where Indy and Griff were chilling. For once, Griff looked relaxed in a pair of shorts and a ratty T-shirt. He normally tried to look like what he called 'artist presentable,' with his collared shirts, rolled up sleeves, and dark wash jeans. If I were in the art department, you wouldn't find me trying so hard. Case in point—Indy. On a regular basis, he looked like he'd just rolled out of bed with his hair sticking out all over, and wrinkled and sometimes hole-y clothes. It seemed to work for him, so why not? But with Griff being as young as he was, and running an academic department, felt compelled to put a little extra pressure on himself.

"Mason, you look like you've seen a ghost," Griff said slowly, his brow furrowing. "What happened? Did you have a near-miss traffic accident or something?"

"Worse… I think I just killed my career," I said, taking a deep breath. "I mean, I knew it could happen. It's not like I'm a robot or something. And I'm still pretty young when you look at things. But I just never…"

"Whoa, whoa, whoa," Indy said, holding up a hand. "Jeez man, take another deep breath. In fact, take like four or five. Remember, you're a communications teacher. Now… communicate."

I did what Indy suggested, and took at least thirty seconds to just breathe in through my nose, then out through my mouth, something I had my students practice on the regular. But as I did, I got another faint whiff of Jessa's perfume, probably clinging to the collar of my shirt. It was a delicious, light scent that had kept me stiff as a board on the short drive home.

Get it together, asshole.

Finally, I could form words. "Something happened as I was leaving campus. I had an incident with a student… maybe two students? I don't know."

Griff sat forward, his face full of concern. "Explain."

"Well, was heading to the gas station, you know the one with that artisanal ginger beer that nobody else stocks," I said.

Indy sometimes would tease me about my hoity-toity taste in ginger beers, but then again, he hadn't spent six months in Australia developing a taste for the stuff. He wasn't joking now, though.

"I hadn't reached my car yet when I heard a girl… yell."

"Yell?" Indy asked. "What kind of yell?"

"The yell that makes the hair stand up on the back of your neck," I said, and they winced. "She yelled no, and you know what that means, so I went to investigate. I found her trying to fight off a guy who seemed not to understand that no literally meant no."

"You intervened?" Indy asked. "Good."

"Yeah well, the little shit might have tried to grab a girl's ass, but he went running like a goddamn pussy when I approached."

Griff chuckled. "And for good reason. Mason, look at you, man. For a teacher, you're a brick shithouse."

I wouldn't have described myself that way. Sure, I was six foot two, but I was only about two hundred pounds give or take. As for any muscularity, that was because I used the campus fitness center four days a week as a way to help deal with the stress of my job. I wasn't trying to intimidate or impress anyone.

"Anyway, he went running, so I checked on her. Turned out she was one of my students. One of my comms students. She was in a panic, angry… a lot of things. I thought everything would be okay, that she was calming down, until… she kissed me."

Indy, who'd been drinking a Budweiser, dropped his beer to the porch, where it clanked loudly and started spreading. "You… kissed her?"

"Well, she kissed me first," I said defensively, realizing how stupid that sounded. "I know it's wrong, but when Jessa laid her kisser on mine—"

"*Jessa?*" Griff asked. "As in *Jessa Carr*? The good-looking girl with the black hair and red lipstick?"

Griff knew her?

"Ah fuck," Indy said, shaking his head as he retrieved his beer. "Okay. I need a fresh one to hear this whole story. I think we're going to need it."

Did he know her too?

Griff hustled for the door. "Be right back. And do not start until I am."

"So… you guys know Jessa Carr?" I asked.

Indy chuckled and nodded slowly. "We'll explain it in a moment. So… did you kiss her back?"

Had these guys fucking kissed her too?

Griff returned with three tumblers and a bottle of bourbon. "Decided we needed something stronger than beer, so I brought out the big guns."

He poured all of us a healthy double shot, then added a little more to mine as I got back to Indy's question.

"I guess I kissed her. I mean, yes. Yes, I did. Although I didn't mean to," I said like a whiny bitch. "She was just… shaken and scared, looking up at me like I was her savior. Then, boom. Her lips were on mine. And… I have to say they were goddamn amazing. I shouldn't say that, I know. It's all kinds of fucked up. You guys know I'm a respected, tenured instructor. I've been around the block. I've never, ever thought about a student that way."

Griff laughed and Indy rolled his eyes.

"Mason, does your dick not work or something?" Griff asked. "Come on, man. I get it, being professional and all. We all try to be professional. But let's be honest. There's about ten *thousand* women between the ages of eighteen and twenty three walking around campus every day. And let's face it, it's a college. These students are literally in the physical primes of their lives. For evolutionary purposes, they are at the top of the desirability heap. Fertile, beautiful, fresh, young. You name it. Tell me, how many students are you carrying this semester?"

I thought quickly, doing the numbers in my head. "About three hundred."

"Okay then. Your senses are assaulted on a daily basis by these women. There's nothing wrong with looking and thinking yeah, she's attractive. My first semester teaching I had a member of the cheerleading squad literally lift her skirt and ask if I could make a silicone mold of her vag."

Point taken.

I threw my hands up. "Okay. Fine. I notice. Everybody does. I've never kissed a student, though. I've never… crossed that line."

Fuck, fuck, fuck.

"Yeah… but Jessa Carr," Indy said dreamily.

I was surprised when Griff nodded along, offering a silent toast. We clinked glasses, and I tossed back most of my shot, relishing the harsh burn of the alcohol in my throat.

"How the hell do you guys know her?" I asked.

"She's an art major," Griff pointed out. "Of course we know her. And yes, she's a once in a lifetime kind of beauty."

"Whom I've seen naked," Indy added with pride, making me choke on the rest of my bourbon. "Well I should say, I saw her in very sheer undies."

"What the fuck?" I coughed, wiping my lips. "What do you mean, you've seen her *naked*?"

I felt badly for kissing her, no doubt, but freaking Indy had seen her *without clothes*? How the hell had that happened? I felt like I'd just landed on an alien planet where I didn't understand the rules.

My mind flooded with thoughts of Jessa, and how she felt pressed against me. And Indy Dawson had seen that body naked?

Fucker.

How was he not up in his room jerking off to thoughts of her at that very moment? Shit, if I'd seen her naked, I probably wouldn't have been able to leave the house for a week.

"How 'bout you start us off, Griff? Fill Mason in, before the man has a goddamn heart attack," Indy suggested.

Griff finished his bourbon. "Okay. So last week, I was in my office when Jessa came by...."

It took us about fifteen minutes to run through the events that led up to Jessa Carr injecting herself into all three of our lives. At least with Griff and Indy, it made sense. She was an art major. Mine was just random freaking chance.

"So in the end," Indy said after we were all caught up, "she kissed you, Mason. I got a full view of everything except her toes, thanks to those clunky army boots. All Griff's gotten so far is a lot of conversation. But promising conversation." He snorted unsympathetically.

I guess it wasn't surprising. We guys were friends and shared a lot of the same interests and values. It wasn't that far out of the realm of possibility that we'd be preoccupied by the same, bewitching woman.

"Sounds like Griff's in the least amount of danger or trouble," I said, taking a deep breath. "Fuck, guys. You know I've got career goals. I'd like to head up the English department some day. Publish a shit ton of books, both academic and fiction. Doing... stuff... with a student is a one way ticket to teaching at some community college."

"At least she isn't in your department," Griff pointed out. "End of this semester, you'll not have to worry about Jessa or her temptations. You'll probably never even see her again. I've got a long, hard road to walk. She's gonna be around for a few years if she decides to get a Master's degree. And as good as her work is, our paths could cross in the art world infinitely."

"I don't feel good about this guys. Not at all," I mumbled.

I guess the best I could do was just make sure it never happened again, and hope like hell word of it never got out.

"I don't know about you guys, but I'm planning on working out more and taking many, many cold showers," Indy said, tossing back the rest of his bourbon. "After all, you might have kissed her, Mason… but I have to spend the rest of the semester seeing her naked for fifty minutes at a pop."

"That's a blessing and a curse if there ever was one," I admitted. The idea of seeing a woman as beautiful as Jessa naked? Heavenly.

Not being able to touch her the whole time? Torture.

"Shit, maybe I'll take your class, Indy," I joked. "I need a new hobby."

He held his arms open wide. "Hey, the more the merrier."

"Look at it this way, Indy," Griff said. "If there's any woman in the world who can inspire a true master-piece? You've got her now."

Indy nodded, and smirked. "Yeah… guess I do, don't I? Truth is, I can barely wait for next Thursday."

He was right. I only had two days until I saw Jessa again, in class… and I was looking forward to it very, very much.

7

JESSA CARR

"So, you know someone at the Kappa fraternity?"

For a lot of people, going to a party on Sunday wasn't a regular thing. But at Wellshire University, and probably any university across the United States, you could find a party of some sort pretty much every day of the week. It just mattered what level of insanity you were open to.

There was always something for everyone.

And with Parents' Weekend putting a damper on the two days per week that were usually free, Sunday night was the best night of my lousy weekend to blow off some steam. And since it was one of Roxy's rare nights off, I had two reasons to go out.

My girl needed a break. And I needed to forget… stuff.

"I don't know anyone at Kappa, but I heard about their party. It's not like there's going to be a doorman checking invites," I said.

I didn't need to say it, but fraternities always wanted more girls. Getting in was never an issue.

And if you were decently cute, the seas parted. College boys were horny, but guys in fraternities took all that to a new level. I'd heard some houses were pretty much 24/7 fucking fests. The more girls the better.

I might have been curvier than Roxy, but she was a whole five alarm smokeshow of her own. She was thinner than me, a bit taller, and was learning to take advantage of every inch she had to show off. I was doing the same of course, but we were two sides of the same coin. The kind of coin that boys pursued, hard.

"So… shall we hit it? C'mon, there will be free beer," I said, surprising myself. I was usually the person who had to be dragged out the door, especially to a frat party.

But Roxy needed further convincing. She clamped her lips closed, shaking her head. "Come on, Jessa, you know that place is a shitshow."

"It is. You are right. But shitshows are good once in a while," I protested. "Please? If only for me?"

She took a deep breath, shrugged, and gave me her stunning smile. Growing up, she didn't have the advantage of orthodontic work, and was left with a sizeable gap in her teeth. I thought it was adorable, and everyone else did, too. But to Roxy it was a chasm the size of the Grand Canyon. Because of it, she almost never smiled. Which was a shame.

"Look, we're going to go have some fun, chill the

fuck out, and then go back to the dorm and sleep. I don't have class until ten tomorrow. I need some party time, even if it is with a bunch of frat bros."

"Fine, I guess," she said, shrugging. "Let's do it."

We walked to the Kappa house, one of the bigger ones on Frat Row. I'd never been tempted to take part in Greek life, myself. It just wasn't my sort of thing. But I had to admit having them close by was great when you were in the mood for a party and didn't want to spend any money.

As I expected, the guys from Kappa were more than happy to see us, and two especially eager dudes immediately volunteered to go get us drinks. Roxy and I turned them down, though. The first thing they taught at freshman orientation was to never take a drink from someone you didn't know. We were used to getting our own, as were all the smart girls around campus.

So we were enjoying the loud tunes and getting into the party when I looked up from sipping my beer. My stomach fell. No, actually, it crashed like a head on collision with a concrete wall.

Across the room, a mere twenty feet away, was Cole, trying to chat up some pretty blonde who was way out of his league.

I don't know why I was so surprised. He had every right to be at the party, just like I did. But I'd just not been… expecting to see him. And I'd not expected to feel this way when I did.

I grabbed Roxy's arm. "Shit. Stick close, would you? Cole's across the room."

"You mean… Cole, the piece of shit you introduced your parents to?" she asked, her lip lifting in a predatory sneer.

I'd told her what happened, leaving out the piece between me and Professor Acker. I was still making up my mind about that, and what, if anything I was going to do about it. And Roxy, for all the middle class privileges she missed out on when growing up, made up for it with a good bit of street smarts. She put up with no crap. Ever. The perfect wing woman. I was safe with her at my side.

"Yeah, that's him," I said, wincing as he caught sight of me. "Fuck."

"He says one bad thing and I'm taking him down," she said.

She'd tried to show me before how to hit someone in the chin with the heel of my hand. I'd never had to do it and didn't know if I successfully could, but I knew she was versed in self-defense. She might look harmless, but cross the woman at your own peril.

I could leave, but I didn't want to run. That wouldn't have helped. Cole would have most likely tracked us through the party like some horror movie villain. Besides, why should I let him chase us out?

So I stood my ground, Rhianna pulsing from the stereo on the other end of the room.

As expected, he wasted no time in swaggering up, looking cocky. "Damn, sugar, you're looking even sexier than yesterday."

Ugh. His breath stank.

"What do you want, Cole?" I growled.

Roxy squared her shoulders and moved closer to me. She was wound tightly, ready to spring.

"What? That you like to play hard to get?" he said, all smarmy smiles. "You like being a cocktease? Well, in case you haven't noticed, I'm not the type to give up easily."

"You mean you're not the type to take a hint," I said. "Jesus, Cole, I was pretty damn clear, wasn't I? Our being together was an *act.* For my parents. You know that."

"Act, huh?" Cole said, turning to Roxy. "She tell you how she was hanging off my arm like we were made for each other? She was practically crawling up my leg, right in front of Mommy and Daddy."

Delusional was what he was. Completely delusional.

Roxy stepped closer to him, and they were nearly eye-to-eye, thanks to her substantial height. "She didn't tell me that, Cole. But she *did* tell me how you tried to go in for privileges that weren't yours." She narrowed her eyes. "*And* how she kicked you."

"I don't mind playing rough."

I sighed, done with his shit. "Get it through your head, Cole. The answer is NO. I'm not interested in you. Never was, and never will be. Especially since I now know what you're all about."

I expected him to yell. I expected him to walk away, maybe. Hell, I expected him to retreat in that typical college boy fashion, saving his pride by acting like I was the one coming on to him.

Instead… he just *smiled*, sending a shiver up my spine. "You should be interested in me, Jessa… so that your parents don't find out about your new 'job.' I'm sure Mommy and Daddy Carr would shit themselves if they learned their artsy-fartsy daughter had signed on to be a nude model. Wonder how that would go down at the *club* your mom spoke so fondly of."

The next few moments of my life were like one of those scenes in the movies, where everything fades away and the camera zooms right in on the character's face. It's called the Vertigo effect or the dolly zoom, or something like that, supposedly invented by Alfred Hitchcock. The whole room dimmed, all sound muffled, and all I could see was Cole's leering face. Bastard knew his words had hit me hard.

"You… wouldn't."

"Why not?" he asked with a nonchalant shrug. "Face it, Jessa, everyone's going to know. You've got half the guys on campus following you around like puppies, trying to sniff your pretty panties, and at least a quarter of the chicks have girl crushes on you, too. You really think that news of you putting those big tits and round ass on display isn't big news?"

"Go to hell," I growled. "I have nothing to apologize for."

"Oh really? Ronald Carr, family patriarch and daddy dearest might feel differently. Lucky for me, because I pretty much charmed his pants off—the man gave me his business card. Said I should call him for a job this summer."

I scoffed, even if I didn't feel very secure in it. "You wouldn't," I said, forcing my chin up, even though I wanted to crawl away.

This was not the way things were supposed to go. Not at all.

"I *wouldn't?*" he taunted.

But before I could say anything more, Roxy intervened, throwing her drink in his face. Heads turned to see what was going on, but Cole smiled through it, wiping his eyes. "It's cool, Jessa. You'll give me what I want. Think about it. I'll be in touch. Oh, and tell Ronald I'll be in touch with him, too. I could use a high-paying summer job where I don't have to do shit except kiss up to the boss."

He sauntered away.

I was so stunned I didn't notice Roxy nudging me. "Hey!" she said, finally shaking me.

"Yeah?" I asked, my air returning in a rush.

"You gonna kick his ass or what?" she asked. "He's trying to blackmail you!"

"I... no. I don't know." I replied. The noise of the party and smell of stale beer were suddenly too much. "Let's get out of here, okay? I'm not feeling this party anymore."

Roxy snagged another cup of beer, chugging it down in three deep swallows, and tossing it to the floor. "Fuck this place. Let's go. It's not like any of these frat fucks would would ever go out with a hotel maid, anyway. Not unless I started looking like prime J-Lo."

The next day, after a fitful night's sleep where I tossed and turned half the night worrying about Cole, Roxy and I met up with Birdie for breakfast. It troubled me that I had to do a double-check of the line to make sure Cole wasn't working in the dining hall.

"You want to talk about it?" Birdie asked when she saw my face. Roxy had filled her in on the party as we dressed back in the dorm room. Birdie had kept her thoughts to herself, listening quietly.

I wasn't ready. "No… please. Let's not. Can we talk about the Spring Show, instead? I need your opinions."

"On what?" Birdie asked as we sat down with our plates.

"Picking my submission for the show," I said, pulling out my phone. "I took pics of what I think are my five best pieces, but I can't decide which belongs at the top of the pile."

I handed my phone over to Birdie and Roxy, who swiped through the photos I'd taken, humming and making little comments about what they liked.

"I like the blue in this one, it makes it happy."

"This one's cool. Really dark and intense."

"Oooh, what about this? Looks like someone was feeling seductive when she did it."

Birdie's last comment kicked off something I'd been dying to ask her about. "Regarding that comment… do you think I could do *more* to get into the show?"

"Like what? What more could you possibly do?" she asked, though her raised eyebrows told me she knew what I was getting at.

Roxy made a face. "No… no way. You'd sleep with a professor to get ahead?"

"Judgmental much?" Birdie said. "You didn't have a problem with me doing it."

"That… that was different," she said quickly, now on thin ice. "Birdie, when you got with your guys, it wasn't… well, you were doing it organically. You liked them. You wanted them for who they were, not because of a grade."

Roxy turned to me. "Birdie is a special case…."

"Hello? I'm sitting right here," Birdie said.

"Well, she has a point," I said. "Your case *is* special. And what you have… it's rare. Three men in love with you, and such good friends themselves, they're not trying to kill each other over you."

"And?"

"Well, that would never happen for me," I said. Still, even as I said it, I thought about something. "But… I did kiss Professor Acker."

What a kiss it was, too. Better than any college guy I'd had, most of whom wanted to fumble around with my mouth before attacking my tits on the way to pressuring me for a blowjob.

Mason Acker's kiss was different. Of course he was

surprised, but for those seconds he kissed me back, it was… more.

Birdie smiled knowingly. "Okay. The truth is coming out."

Roxy just sat with her mouth open.

"Yeah, but there are complications. Lots of them. I'm ninety nine percent sure Dad's going to cut me off if I don't play his game. You know, of finding a husband. And with Cole on the war path, I am so fucked."

Roxy shook her head. "That is such bullshit. And what will you do if a husband doesn't suddenly appear on the horizon?"

"*Hello.* That's what I'm getting at. That's why I'm so desperate to get into the Spring Show. If I win, that means I'm set, at least to a point. And I'll do anything to get in. Anything."

8

GRIFF LEDGER

I TURNED LEFT, heading down the hall towards the painting lab that was the site of my next class. It was Advanced Color Theory, a course that had me thinking not so much about the dozen students I had waiting for me, but about a student from a previous semester... the lovely Jessa Carr.

Indy and Mason had their moments with her. They'd seen her, felt her... tasted her. All I'd had was a conversation. I couldn't blame them for liking her, or for being tempted by her. I was in the same boat.

She was different. Not just because of her stunning looks. Not because of the fact that sensual energy oozed from every pore of her skin. Not because of the fact that despite her inherent sexiness, she wasn't intentionally using it like currency to buy her way through life.

No. She was dedicated to art. She wasn't just some spoiled pretty girl looking to have a good time in college. I'd reviewed her records, read her teacher evaluations. The truth was, she was an overlooked gem. Every teacher talked about her talent, about her eye for art, and her vision.

But none had sponsored her for the Spring Show. I suspected I knew why. Ironically, Jessa Carr might have been *too* beautiful. Professors, trying to not be influenced by her incomparable good looks, chose to honor other students so as not to appear biased.

An ironic twist, considering I did the same thing when she was my student.

Up ahead I heard a light commotion, and saw Jessa Carr herself walking down the hallway, it looked like maybe towards the lower floor painting labs. She wasn't making noise of course, it was the five guys who were either following her or calling out to her like she was a pop star. What was it the college kids were calling it? Thirsty?

Those five were as thirsty as someone stranded in the Sahara for five days.

Jessa paused, chatting with one of the guys for a minute, and I shocked myself by feeling a twinge of jealousy. What the hell was that about? The truth was, I had an urge to walk a little faster, to catch up with her and strike up a conversation myself, but that was ridiculous. Besides, what if the guy she was talking to was her boyfriend?

Then again, would she have kissed Mason if she did have one? Maybe. People do weird things when they are scared. And I was an art professor, not a psychologist.

I got through class and back to my office, where I reviewed an e-mail for the department admin to send. It was a form letter to all the entrants for the Spring Show, thanking them for applying. There were a record number of applicants this year, everyone is super talented, blah blah blah. I wrapped it up by saying that the final selections were upcoming, and that's when I'd send an email again, with all final decisions.

I'd just hit send to forward it to my assistant when there was a knock on my door. "Come in," I called.

"Professor Ledger? It's me, Jessa."

The door opened all the way, and she entered my office. She was… a dream. Her top that day was loose, billowy and black, a top that I'd seen girls wear in dance clubs. It was an absolute genius in clothing design, loose enough to give the impression that at any moment, she might reveal a heart-stopping perfect curve of breast… and yet as she walked she never did.

"Jessa," I said, blinking as I heard the click of my office door latch. She crossed the small space and leaned over my desk, giving me a view down her blouse.

Perfection.

It was the only way to describe the sight before my eyes. I was a decent artist, not as good as Indy, but no slouch. Still, I knew in that instant that there was no way I could ever, even if I lived to be a thousand years old, create an image as beautiful and sensual as the sight of Jessa Carr looking at me, her pink lips soft, her eyes burning with unknown energy, her chin leading my eyes down to the view of her soft, full, rounded breasts. Her nipples were stiff, and my mouth went dry as I realized she was trying to seduce me.

I should have said no.

I should have been professional.

But instead I just looked, as firmly caught as a fish on a hook.

"Professor… Griff, I need your help," Jessa said. "I found my piece, and I want to show it to you."

I nodded numbly and she bit her lip, standing up to reach into the waistband of her skirt to withdraw a piece of folded up paper. She handed it to me, and I swore as I unfolded it I could smell…

My god, it was the scent of her pussy. Almost all the blood left my brain to rush to my dick as the thought hit me, and I looked at the picture in my hands, a photograph of a painting.

"It's… good," I said, unable to form words more articulate than that. In the tiny part of my brain *not* thinking about Jessa and her beauty, I had to admit it was more than good. It was a study in sensuality that was better than any piece I'd ever produced.

But I couldn't say that. All I could think about was how sexy she was, how I knew what she was trying to do, what I should be doing… and what I couldn't resist.

"Is it good enough to get into the Spring Show?" she purred, and I nodded, dumbly.

"Yes. Very good."

Jessa smiled, and my erection strained against the confines of my blue jeans. I'd made this angel smile, and my cock was happy about it.

"Thank you," she said, her fingers pushing down on the zipper on the side of her skirt.

Jesus. She was going for it.

It slipped off her hips down her legs, where it pooled on the floor of my office. That's when I found she was wearing underneath… nothing at all.

"Jessa—"

"Shhhhh," she said, putting a finger to my lips. "I know. I want this. I want to thank you, and… I want *you.*"

She wanted me. Those three words pierced through any paper-thin defenses I could have mustered, and when she pulled her top over her head to reveal the total perfection of her body, I became a man without conscious thought.

I was all instinct. Instinct that made me stand up, pull her close and kiss her. She wrapped her arms around my neck eagerly, kissing me back, and I was goddamn lost. My hands roamed over her body, exploring every inch I could reach as our lips and tongues tasted each other.

"Griff…" she whispered in my ear, repeating again, "I want you."

All I could do was growl in reply as I lifted her in my arms, setting her on my desk. I roughly pushed her knees apart, my eyes going to the juncture of her thighs. Her pussy was just as pale as I imagined, the lips a lily white flushed with a touch of pink, silky smooth and tasty looking.

Best of all, I could see the gleaming wetness at the center of her slit, and the way her clit was peeking out of its hood at the top, showing me that yes… yes, she was aroused. I leaned down, kissing up the inside of her thigh as her eyes found mine, and she looked at me with eager trepidation.

"You're… going to?" she asked, and I nodded.

Fuck yeah, I was going to.

I smiled, and reached out with my tongue. I took my time, licking her from bottom to top before doing it again, relishing the magical taste of her wetness. Her eyes rolled back at the sensation, and a little part of me was proud.

Nobody'd ever licked her pussy before, or if they had, they hadn't done it right. This knowledge fueled my passion and I dove in, licking, sucking, tasting. She was tangy and delicious, sensitive to my lips and tongue as I explored every fold, nibbling at her soft skin before zeroing in on her clit.

"Oh fuck!" she gasped, her back arching as I flicked my tongue over her bud. "Oh yes, right there, yes, I'm gonnaaaaaa…."

Her voice went raspy, and her legs wrapped around my head as she came all over my tongue, flooding my mouth with her sweet juices. I took it in until she sagged on my desk and I stood up, freeing myself from my jeans and boxers.

She looked down, her eyes widening when she saw me. "You… you eat pussy and are hung like that?" she asked, blinking as I took myself in hand and stroked my length. "Are you sure you're human?"

"Turn over," I growled, my first words since I'd said her name. She nodded, placing her boot-clad feet on the ground. She pushed off the desk enough that I could see her breasts dangle on their own as I grabbed her waist.

My cock was so hard it hurt, and after sheathing myself with a condom I'd pulled from my jeans pocket, I entered her with one long, slow stroke. I could see her tense as she expected me to just skewer her, but the pleasure of my slow thrust made her push back into me, arching until I could cup a perfect breast and kiss her neck.

It wasn't hard to go slow, as much as I wanted to ravage her. But the same instinct that said I needed this woman also held me back, saying I wanted her more than once. So I didn't just pound her. I thrust deep, grinding and pleasing her, my hand massaging her breast and tugging on her nipple until she turned her head to look back at me, her eyes full of passion.

I claimed her. Slowly we moved together, letting our bodies join and rise together. Time stopped having meaning as we sped up and slowed, her hips pushing back into my thrusts and her arms grabbing the edge of my desk as she leaned forward, taking me deeper and deeper.

I felt her tremble as I swelled, and I knew I couldn't

hold back much longer. I didn't care and sped up, my hips finally slapping against her as she clenched and rolled with me, chasing her own release.

With a soft gasp, she came again and I crested, my fingers clamping tightly around her waist as I thrust hard, exploding in the biggest orgasm of my life. What felt like a gallon of cum erupted from my cock and I shook, the world graying out as I stayed buried inside her the entire time.

"Mmmm… oh my god," she said. "I didn't know if you'd… be receptive to my advances."

"You're too sexy to resist," I admitted as I pulled out, glistening with her juices.

She turned to face me and smiled, bending down to softly suck me clean. It was glorious torture, and by the time she was finished, my cock was half hard again.

"Jessa—"

"Shhhh, Griff," she said, standing up. She looked into my eyes, biting her lip. "Like I said, I wanted to. I wanted you. I hope we can do this again."

I didn't answer. Of course I wanted to fuck her again. But something was trying to talk me out of it. Hard.

She grabbed her skirt and top. Within seconds she was dressed, and from somewhere in her things she'd produced a pair of panties.

She came up to me, put her arms around my neck, and kissed me again. "I'm looking forward to the e-mail about the Spring Show… and our next meeting.

And I promise, outside your office I'll remember to call you Professor."

"I hope so," I said, and she gave me one last angel's smile before she left.

With numb legs, I sat back in my office chair, still in shock at what had just happened.

Her fucking me was clearly a quid pro quo. She wanted something, so she gave me something.

I wasn't complaining. She didn't know it yet, but she was already in the goddamn show. That's how good she was.

I was going to ensure our next tryst was one where we wanted each other only, with no distractions hanging over our heads.

I wanted her, and she wanted me. She just might not know it yet.

9

JESSA CARR

I STOOD in my dorm room, looking in my closet and trying to figure out what to wear. On one hand, I felt totally ridiculous. I was getting ready for my first modeling gig, where I was going to get naked. I could wear a ball gown, or I could wear a bathrobe, it didn't really matter. I was going to take it off and no one would even see it.

Idiot.

But it did matter. For some reason a little thing like this felt massively important. I was nervous enough as it was, after everything that had happened so fast... stripping for Professor Dawson, kissing Professor Acker... having sex with Griff.

Jesus. What was happening to me?

I hadn't specifically gone to Griff's office with the intention of fucking him. Well, not totally. I figured I could tease him a little. I'd left my panties off as a last minute personal dare. But after kissing Professor

Acker, something unlocked inside me. Seeing the desire in his eyes had me going with a vibe that was… amazing.

Professors had it all over stupid little college boys. There was no doubt about it.

But now I was nervous. Could I still earn a spot in the Spring Show on my own merit? Had I ruined an opportunity to show my talent?

Kind of late to be worrying about that.

With trembling fingers I picked out a simple T-shirt and a pair of black jeans, opting for something I could change in and out of easily. But on a last second impulse, I traded in the T-shirt for a hooded tee. The loose cotton covering most of my upper body was strangely comforting.

I started doing my makeup, trying for something not too crazy. Would they even be drawing my face? I actually had no idea. But I wanted to look good.

The door opened and Birdie flew in, looking fabulous as ever. Every day that she was with her three men, she grew as a woman and as a world class beauty.

"Well now. Guess I arrived just in time," she said.

"What do you mean?" I asked, capping my lipstick. "Something wrong?"

"You're anxious. I can see it in your face," she said, propping her little butt on the edge of the bathroom sink. "And you never wear that shirt unless you're nervous. The last time I saw it was when you thought you were about to fail math."

I looked down at my shirt, and had to admit she was

right. Regardless of the time of year, this was my 'blankie' top. But what difference did it make? Some people had a lucky necklace or other talisman. This shirt was mine.

"Maybe I'm a little nervous," I said casually.

"Why?" Birdie said. "Jessa, you're fucking *gorgeous*. You're confident, you're badass… hell, for the first year we were rooming together I always looked up to you. I mean, I was the shy girl library nerd, you were this vivacious babe. I wanted to be like you."

Now I want to be like you, I thought. *Already had sex with a professor, too.*

"So, you looked up to me your first year. Does that mean you now look down on me?" I laughed.

She playfully slapped my arm. "You know what I mean, you dork."

"I'm a teeny bit nervous about the drawing class. But that coupled with the issues I'm having with my parents, and that creep, Cole, are what's really weighing on me," I said.

"I get it. That Cole is a fucker. We'll figure out what to do about him. Just keep going about your business like the fabulous bitch you are, and all will be well."

I wished I had the confidence in myself that Birdie did.

"Look," she continued, "you're going to be a natural model and inspire great art. On that note, have you heard anything yet about the Spring Show?"

"Nope. Waiting for the coveted email," I said.

"They're about to announce semi-finalists, and then finalists after that."

What if my sleeping with Griff had actually ruined my chances with the show? Why hadn't I considered that before I went in there and took all my clothes off?

God, I was stupid.

If I'd fucked myself over like I suspected I might have, then the scholarship was dead in the water.

That couldn't happen. It just couldn't.

If I didn't have my shit lined up before Cole pulled the trigger on his threat, or before my parents realized he was a fake boyfriend and cut me off, I'd be totally fucked. It would all be over.

Just before I left, Birdie pulled me in tight for a hug. "Come on now, just hug me, and breathe."

Hugs. Such simple human contact, but exactly what I needed. Birdie's arms helped me pull myself together, at least enough to not have a breakdown right there in my dorm room.

"Thank you, Birdie," I said.

"Anytime. Look, I know you, babe. You're on that fucking Spring Show list," she said, and I had to smile a little.

Oh, I was on a fucking list all right, just not the one Birdie was talking about.

She continued her pep talk. "Now, there's probably some committee that has to horse trade, stroke egos, and all that shit. They just need to do their thing, add the other names so that all the right people can have their egos massaged just the way they want. Relax."

I nodded, and with Birdie's help I finished getting ready. I walked quickly from the dorm towards the art building, ignoring the looks and calls I got when I usually crossed campus. Despite Birdie's encouragement, I was still shaky, my knees knocking as I got to the room, where I found Professor Dawson setting things up for class.

"Jessa," he greeted me, giving me an evaluating look. "You ready for today?"

I nodded, even if I didn't quite feel confident. I walked over to a corner and put my bag down, reaching for the hem of my t-shirt. I had it three quarters of the way off when he cleared his throat.

"Ahem… Jessa?"

"Yes, Professor Dawson?"

I lifted the piece of hood that had fallen in front of my eyes, blowing a lock of hair out of my face.

He pointed to a corner, where I saw a cloth screen. "First, call me Indy like I asked, and second, we have an area for you to dress in. Right behind that screen. You can leave your things there, too."

"Oh. Right. Thank you, Indy."

I blushed, embarrassed I was so much a rookie that I didn't even think to ask how things worked. Tugging my shirt back down, I took my things behind the screen and stripped before pulling on the cotton robe someone had hung on a hook for me.

I heard the students arrive, my hands shaking as I sat on the dressing area stool and listened. I was such an idiot. I was going to fuck this up, I was going to get kicked out of school, I was…

"Jessa, it's time," Indy said, coming over. "We're ready for you."

Stepping out in front of those students was surreal. Getting naked for Indy? Easy. Thrilling, in fact. I knew I'd been aroused.

Getting naked with Griff before we had sex? Even more arousing.

Stepping out in front of a dozen or so art students while wearing that robe? Absolutely fucking terrifying.

I saw the spot I was supposed to pose on, and the wooden chair that was set up for me. Taking a deep breath I walked over to it and untied my robe. My hands shook, but looking at Professor Dawson helped me. He gave me a small nod and I slid my robe off my shoulders, laying it across the back of the chair before striking the same pose I'd done for my tryout.

Within minutes, I was falling apart. The pose was harder than I thought it would be—it had been years since my last ballet lesson. And with the strain came the shakes, and I could feel myself move, causing students to groan.

I heard my phone buzz, earning more groans.

"For fuck's sake," one of the students grumbled, a guy by the sound of it.

He was right to be irritated. There was a standing rule in art labs. Phones off. Not silent. *Off.* But I was so shaken, so distracted, I'd forgotten.

I went to get my phone, earning more groans. I

knew I was fucking up, but I switched it off as quickly as I could.

"Sorry," I mumbled to the class.

I went back, reassuming my pose, but it was agony. My muscles weren't ready to hold the position, and I could feel cramps threatening my arms and calves. I hadn't even prepped myself properly. Instead of an electrolyte rich light meal, I'd sucked down coffee with breakfast, two big cups of dark richness that might have woken me up… but now left me with a desperate urge to pee.

Don't pee on your leg, don't pee on your leg, don't pee on your—

Across from me, a female student rolled her eyes, and I found something to focus on—her. That bitch didn't understand what I was going through. She didn't understand that I was scared out of my fucking mind, that I was swimming in a sea of emotions she had no concept of. All she knew was that I was Wellshire University's 'alt girl,' the one who supposedly had it easy because I had a string of guys ready to get into my pants at any instant.

She didn't know about Cole. She didn't know about the terror of his threats, or of my parents not paying for school.

None of them did.

Finally, the torture came to an end. I said nothing as I sagged into the chair, my body so exhausted I didn't care that I wasn't sitting at all in a ladylike fashion, nor that I was still naked. These people had already been looking at my tits and ass for nearly an hour. What was a quick look at my vag going to do?

When everyone was gone, I leaned on the chair, pushing myself to my feet. My arms tingled and my toes were chilly from the floor, but at least none of those judgmental jerks could see me limp to the screen, where I could put my clothes on and have a quiet moment to break down in peace.

"Jessa."

I paused, my robe around my shoulders but unbelted. It was Indy, standing by the window, his eyes looking at me darkly. I turned to face him, fear in my throat.

I was so getting fired. I knew it. I was the worst model in the history of art class models, and I probably wasn't even getting paid for the one session I'd managed.

Swallowing my fear, I turned to him as bravely as I could. "Yes, Indy?"

He cleared his throat and stepped forward. "We need to talk."

Yup. I was so getting fired.

10

INDY DAWSON

She stood there, tired and vulnerable... and more beautiful than she had been the entire previous hour. With the thin robe hanging off her shoulders, a remnant from some previous professor's closet no doubt, she was beyond exhausted. I wanted to take her into my arms and tell her the world was going to be okay.

She was a tired goddess, holding my attention in full force.

Fuck me. I knew Mason and Griff were both drawn to her. Hell, the way Griff had acted the other day, I suspected he and Jessa had maybe had another encounter that consisted of more than just conversation.

But in that instant, I didn't care. If my friends wanted Jessa Carr, that was fine... and I wanted her too. But still, I was freaking out. She was just...

standing there, looking at me, more enchanting than if Venus herself had come down from Olympus and presented herself as a gift.

"Um," I said, trying to find words and failing. I licked my lips, and let out a deep breath. "Jessa, you can get dressed now."

I hoped she'd follow my instructions so that, maybe, I could actually think with a clear head. Instead, she stepped forward, her eyes filled with worry and pain and more. She took my hand.

"Please, Indy, I know I messed up," she said, holding my hand as she pleaded. "I know I did badly. But I can't lose this job… I can't. I'm already struggling and… oh god, this would be a nail in my coffin. Please, I can't—"

Her words broke off and a tear slipped down her cheek. Without even thinking, I reached out, maybe to pat her on the shoulder, maybe just to reassure her. I wasn't sure. Instead, I found myself with my arms around her, her body pressed against mine.

It was unexpected, but not unwelcome. It was almost natural, the way she wrapped her arms around me and I, in return, stroked her hair. She tilted her face up to me and I looked down into those beautiful eyes, and without a word passing between us, we were kissing.

Jessa Carr's kiss was everything any man could have wished for. I had the perfect woman in my arms, and as our kiss deepened we found ourselves moving together. I pushed her back and turned, sitting on the stool behind the dressing screen, and pulled her down to straddle my hips.

I gathered her in my arms and kissed down her throat, tracing its curve with the tip of my tongue as my hands explored her ass. It was the ideal bottom, soft yet firm, and as I kneaded her flesh I found myself wanting to explore every inch of her, to try every nerve, to see what pleasures I could bring her... and what pleasures she could bring me.

Jessa leaned back, and I buried my face in the swell of her breasts. I knew they were large and sweet, but the feeling of her silky smooth skin against my lips, and the way she moaned when my tongue found her nipple, was more than I'd anticipated. Even her scent, a soft aroma of pure, clean soap, all heady and herbal, added to my arousal.

I sucked greedily, pulling her tighter as her hips ground down against my crotch, my dick painfully hard in my jeans. I switched from breast to breast, not letting her adjust to my ministrations. I varied my pressure and touch, tugging one moment, teasing with my tongue the next. I wanted to fully experience her, to learn her and to absorb every sound she could make.

She trembled, emotions and desire swirling together as I reached between her legs and found her slick wetness, and the rock hard nub at the top. She was baby smooth, and as my fingers stroked her lips I marveled at how a woman who clearly exercised enough to stay in phenomenal shape was so... soft.

Everywhere, but especially over the tulip petals of her pussy, she was soft and yielding.

She was a dream.

"Yessss," she moaned as I stroked her clit while biting on her right nipple. I smiled, looking up into her eyes. She reached between us, finding the waistband of my jeans in the tangle of legs, hips, arms and bodies between us, and undid the button.

I knew what she wanted, and lifted her in my arms. I wanted it too. She stood just long enough to undo my zipper and free me. I barely had a chance to relish the feeling of her fingers stroking me before I sheathed myself and she pushed me back down on the stool to lower herself.

I impaled her pussy to the hilt.

"Fuck," I gasped, and Jessa smiled, a devilishly angelic smile that said she knew what she was doing to me... and that she liked it. She clenched her muscles around me and I nearly came right there. It was only the desire to see this angel come for me that kept me from blowing my entire load in that instant. Instead, I smacked her ass lightly, smiling up at her.

"Do it baby. Ride my cock."

They were the only words we exchanged as she took over, grinding hard and fast. Her pussy tightened and relaxed around me in time with her strokes, massaging me and igniting a fire inside that had me burning up in seconds.

We both knew the danger, that at any moment someone might come to the drawing lab and hear the commotion we were making behind the dressing screen. That danger just added to our passion. We became a pair, both of us taking and giving with equal measure as we searched for the release we both needed.

Jessa leaned in, kissing me hard and deep, and in seconds we exploded, our bodies pulsing with pleasure as I came inside her perfect body. I could feel myself pouring into her, my hands clamped on her ass as I held her balls deep and I got to watch her shake, her breath coming in little hitched gasps as her breasts flushed pink and her thighs clamped my hips.

I'd never forget the sight of her.

When it was over, she stroked my face, kissing me again. "Thank you. I... you made me feel... so beautiful."

"You *are* beautiful, Jessa," I told her honestly. "And... don't worry about your modeling session. It wasn't the worst I've seen."

"So I've still got a job?" she said, giggling lightly.

This wasn't about trading sex for a modeling gig. I wasn't running some art department casting couch. And I wasn't going to cheapen what just happened between us by tying it to her posing job.

"Yeah, you've got a job still. This has nothing to do with that."

"Thank you." It was just two words, but it said a lot. Instead of replying, I pulled her in for another kiss, this one softer and more tender. This wasn't me telling her she was a sexy woman, or that I wanted to fuck her brains out.

This was a kiss of affection. A kiss that I hoped told her that whatever was on her mind, whatever was going on in her world, I would be there for her. She kissed me back, and that was enough. She knew, and I knew.

Jessa began to dress, her skin still flushed, but the evidence of our passion was at least covered now.

"So… next time, Professor?"

"Yeah, next time," I told her, standing up and tucking my dick back in my boxers. I was still so rocked I'd barely moved. "But please, when we're alone, call me Indy?"

Her smile was more than worth the danger of what my offer implied. "Okay, Indy. See you later."

She left the lab, and I went over to the sink on the wall that was normally used by watercolor students to rinse out their brushes and clean up at the end of class. I splashed water on my face, marveling at what just happened. I'd violated a bunch of university rules, and probably the trust Griff had placed in me.

Truth was, I didn't regret a damn bit of it. A woman like Jessa? She was worth any risk possible, and seeing the smile on her face made it all worth it.

Once I was reasonably put together, minus the wet spot on my jeans from Jessa's pussy juices that I covered up with my AC/DC T-shirt, I walked back to my office. While I didn't like using the space considering how tight it was, I did need to check my e-mails, and I didn't carry a laptop around everywhere.

What I got when I opened my messages left me furious.

Dear Mr. Dawson,

This letter is to inform you that your current position, under the Cronenberg Visiting Scholar program, will be coming to an end with the end of the current semester. Wellshire University appreciates all that you have done to contribute to the university and...

I read the rest of it at light speed, knowing it was just bureaucratic, ass covering bullshit. Then again, I should have anticipated it. Griff was able to get me a slot at the university because he'd used the loophole of the Visiting Scholar program. I'd already stayed beyond the initial grant.

The program wasn't under Griff's control. He'd warned me about that. Sure, he kept trying to get me to settle down, to find a permanent position with the university. But I was really only interested in the art department, and I was still working on it.

But maybe it was for the best. I didn't get into art to be a teacher. And while professor life was fine for Griff, I wasn't sure I was cut out for it on a long-term basis.

Now was time to proverbially shit or get off the pot. I had until the end of the semester to make up my mind about what to do next. Even then I wasn't assured of getting a spot. Griff bitched constantly about the tight budget the fine arts department had, and how he was constantly fighting the university for more money.

So even if I landed an instructor position, it might not be a permanent gig.

It was time to get my ass in gear. I had the rest of the semester to produce some good work, and reach out to my network about gallery opportunities.

There had to be someone out there who thought a thirty-four year old badass with a penchant for rock band T-shirts still had an eye and a vision worthy of sharing with the world.

11

JESSA CARR

"Next up… Jessa Carr."

I was a phony. Plain and simple

From the first moment I walked onto campus at Wellshire University, I'd done things my way. I'd taken on college life by giving exactly zero fucks about what was expected of me, and followed my own path.

Combat boots? Check. I had two pairs in fact, one all leather black and the other a tan jungle boot style.

Tops that had no problem emphasizing my boobs while at the same time saying they weren't there for just anyone and their brother to ogle? Check. Bustier tops, tank tops, T-shirts—didn't matter. I dressed to make myself feel sexy and badass.

Skirts, shorts, or even jeans that had edge to them? Damn right. Even when I was trying to look nice, or in the middle of winter, I kept my punk-ish motif.

But today, that Jessa Carr was nowhere to be seen. No, today's Jessa Carr was wearing a modest cranberry colored blouse borrowed from Birdie, a professional pencil skirt found on sale at a big box store... and Mom's pearls.

Call it the family jewels, that's what my mother did as she joked about sending them to me for good luck. Because even Mom knew that my speech in today's Comms class was important. She could be supportive when she wanted to.

Professor Mason Acker's class. Speech Communications. It was strange, really. I could express myself in paints easily. In normal conversation, I never had any problems getting my point across. I could monologue on subjects for hours, it seemed like.

But tell me to make a prepared five minute speech on a topic? I was a babbling mess.

Normally I could skate by. Not perfectly, and not even very well, but I could get by. If I had to accept a C in the class because of my non-existent public speaking talent, so be it.

This time though, a C wouldn't cut it. The Spring Show required we students show 'excellent standards' in more than just art. And while Griff might have said my piece was good enough, that didn't guarantee me a slot, and it surely didn't mean I would win. I had to nail this speech to make sure my grades were excellent enough for the committee.

When my turn came, I stood, smoothing my pencil skirt over my ass as I walked toward the steps leading to the podium. We were in an auditorium classroom, a cavernous space normally reserved for those massive freshman grinder classes like Psych 101. The fact that we had all this space, and only twenty students, made the auditorium seem that much bigger. And empty. And kind of depressing, when you got right down to it. But give me a full auditorium or an intimate class of twenty, and I still had to try not to stumble on the three steps to the podium, that's how much my knees were knocking.

I was such a poseur. A big, fat, fake. Who was I to be up in front of a group, trying to give a speech on a subject I not only wasn't an expert in, but also, knew nothing about?

"Thank you," I said into the microphone, clearing my throat. "My subject today is about the difference between NFL and college football overtime rules, and which, if either should—"

The microphone popped and squealed, making me wince. There were a few titters in the audience, which I could barely see because of the bright lights in my face.

How did I even get this subject? I didn't know shit about football outside of it being pretty much the biggest example of dick-waving at Wellshire University. No other activity could get twenty thousand guys together in one location to act like total animals all over some macho display of aggression that was purely heterosexual… yet started with one man sticking his hands between another man's legs while wearing skin-tight pants.

"So, ah… the current system of overtime rules in football, ah…" I stumbled before the microphone popped again, causing me to recoil and lose my place. I looked down at my speech, and couldn't see where I'd left off.

Ten seconds in and already an unmitigated disaster. Why didn't I come dressed as myself, and why couldn't I have gotten a subject I was even a little interested in? Why'd I come looking like some corporate PR chick? Why did I have to pick that particular topic out of the fucking hat?

"—and so, yeah… like, that's why the NFL overtime rules suck."

I didn't know how I'd gotten to the end. The past five minutes were a blank. All I knew was that I'd fucked it up. Even looking at Mason's face, that handsome face I'd kissed, I could tell I was in trouble. He was disappointed, and that stung worse than any grade.

Without even waiting for the rest of the speeches to conclude, I rushed from the auditorium and went back to my dorm room, trying not to cry. When I arrived, Birdie was there, sitting at her desk for once and studying.

"What the… hey, how was it?" she asked as I slammed my door behind me. "That bad, huh?"

"It was a fucking disaster," I growled, yanking my ridiculous heels off to throw them into my wardrobe as hard as I could. "Never fucking wearing *those* things again!"

"Okay."

"What… what are you doing here, anyway?" I asked,

trying to control my nerves since my next move would have been to yank my pearls off.

"I needed some quiet reading time," Birdie admitted with a chuckle, "and the library was out of the question since I work there. People are constantly interrupting me. But it's okay. I was mostly done anyway. Do you know how hard it is to try and digest Jay Gatsby and the rest of the self-centered, shallow characters that Fitzgerald writes about, when you've got a sexy as fuck Kai lying in bed next to you, looking ripe for a session of sucky fucky?"

No, I didn't know what that was like. Not by any stretch of the imagination.

I took another deep breath, and shook my head. Yeah, I'd be distracted by him too, with his hot Prince Harry vibe.

"So tell me about your speech," Birdie said. "I don't even know the subject."

"Football overtime rules," I said, and Birdie laughed. "I know, right? What the fucking fuck? Is that actually a topic *anyone* is interested in?"

"Let me guess, random draw?" she asked, and I nodded. "Damn. Why didn't you try and change?"

"I was too focused on my art classes and the Spring Show." I offered. "I should have tried harder to trade with someone. I'm sure one of the dudes in the class would have loved to drone on about something having to do with sports. Anyway, I figured how hard could it be? I thought I could handle it. But then all this shit with my parents and Cole and... other stuff happened.

I didn't put the time in I should have and now I'm probably fucked because a less than stellar grade knocks me out of eligibility for the Spring Show."

I pulled on my beloved tattered bathrobe, the one that Birdie and Roxy gave me shit over, and dove into my bed, prepared to stay there for the rest of the semester.

"Okay. You're upset and pissed off," Birdie said, standing up and coming over. "Who are you mad at? Yourself? Professor Acker?"

"No! Mason… it's not his fault!" I said, and Birdie lifted an eyebrow at my use of his first name. But I continued before she could start asking questions. "I'm pissed at my parents! At Cole! At… at myself!"

She took a seat on the edge of my bed, and I scooted over to make room for her.

She patted my arm. "You can't control being pissed at your parents or Cole. If anything, they deserve it. And as for the speech, it's done. You can't change how you did. So you need to move forward."

Easy for her to say.

"Maybe but… it was bad. I stuttered, I stumbled… I think I said NBA instead of NFL at one point."

Birdie winced. "Ouch."

"If I fuck this up, the committee will keep me out of the Spring Show," I told her. "I mean, I have my job 'helping' out in the department," I said with air quotes, "as well as Griff's nomination. But the committee is more cut and dry… I need top grades."

"I have an idea. Could you pull this speech off if you

had another chance? Look, I know you can talk about art for an hour or more. You make even Picasso interesting."

"You don't like me talking about art?" I asked.

She waved her hands around. "Not the point. What I'm saying is, that when you talk about art, you're exploding with passion. Even talking about brush strokes or color choices sounds interesting. And there are other subjects you can talk about that are edge of your seat interesting. You can be very persuasive."

"Like?"

"Like when you talked me into revealing I was a virgin in an English paper?" she pointed out. "Very convincing. Very life-changing."

I nodded, touched. "You were pissed at the time… for a little bit."

"Yeah, well, good speeches can piss people off and still get plenty of reaction," she pointed out. "Jessa, here's what you need to do. Get your ass out of bed and get out of that rag of a robe you're wearing. Put on your Jessa clothes. I want you to look like the crazy, badass friend I know and love."

She stood and extended a hand, practically yanking me off the bed.

"Then, you'll go talk to Professor Acker. Go in there as the total royal babe you are, and show him that you can deliver a speech that would charm anyone, even if it is about freaking football. Tell him you want another chance, and that you'll do what's necessary to get your grade up."

She was right. I needed to talk with Mason. I meant, Professor Acker. I pulled on my 'real' clothes, and instantly felt better.

"Oh… one last thing."

"What?"

"Lose the pearls."

12

MASON ACKER

ONE... two... three... four... five... six... seven.

For whom did the bell toll?

Perhaps, I thought with a chuckle, it tolled for me. After all, it was seven in the evening, well after my last class of the day, and I was still sitting in my office, plowing through a series of English papers for one of my freshman classes. It was taking forever.

I could have been like most of my colleagues and done the work at home. More than once I'd gotten a memo or note from someone with a smear of ketchup or ringlet of wine on a corner. But for most of this semester, I didn't want to work at home.

It wasn't that Griff or Indy were bad housemates. If anything, they were too good as roommates, if that was even possible. Instead of spending all my time in the guest cottage out back, only going into the main house to do laundry on the weekends, I was continually tempted to hang out with them. Even when I had other things to do.

It was just too easy. We'd sit around for hours on the porch, or in Griff's living room if the weather was bad, talking. Sometimes they were serious talks, where the three of us discussed and debated issues of the day. Other times, we'd just flap our gums. Having a three man Super Bowl party the previous year had been a blast. It was awesome having friends like that, something I hadn't had in a long time.

But friendships didn't get my papers graded. And while I knew Griff and Indy both had 'regular' assignments for their students, they had more time to hang out at the house and chill while I slogged my way through essays.

I was trying to force myself through another student's paper, when there was a knock on my office door. I looked up, blinking against the darkness of my office outside my desk lamp. I hadn't even noticed the sun go down.

"Yes?" I called.

"Professor Acker… it's me, Jessa Carr."

Shit.

I knew what protocol said. It was outside office hours, outside business hours even, and she was an attractive female student while I was alone in my office. I should have told her to come back the next day, when I was 'safe.'

But those concerns evaporated as I remembered the pain in her eyes when she fumbled through her speech earlier in the day… and the feeling of her kiss the week before.

I took a deep breath. I was taking a calculated risk. "Come in, Jessa."

I was expecting the professionally-outfitted Jessa who flubbed her speech that afternoon. I had no idea who'd dressed her like that, but it plain hadn't worked. Instead of giving her the confidence she thought she lacked, it had made her lose her stride. But now, the girl who came through my door was the real thing. She was wearing a satin bustier top that left her already curvy body dramatically more voluptuous, with her narrow waist flaring out to sexy hips clad in black denim. She looked stunning, her black hair brushed back and her lips darkened.

Under my desk, I felt something stir. This was the Jessa I'd kissed the other night, right down to the combat boots that were half-laced, like she was ready to kick ass. This Jessa was feeling her mojo, her power… her feminine sexuality.

I liked it.

"I want another chance," she said without preamble. "I know I can do that speech."

I'd been expecting that. "Jessa, your grade isn't so poor that you need to—"

"I need it for the Spring Show," she said, interrupting me. Thumping her hands on my desk she fixed me with her eyes, and to be honest I couldn't tear my gaze away even if I'd wanted to. Seeing she had my attention, she stood up, actually taller than me since I was seated, her eyes never wavering from mine.

She dove in. "Overtime in American football has become a matter of discussion and debate in many sports circles," she intoned, her voice strong and powerful and strident. "But it wasn't always so. The NFL didn't have any form of overtime until 1940, and the first official game to go to overtime was the 1958 NFL Championship between the Giants and the Colts. Meanwhile, college football didn't have any kind of overtime until 1995. That overtime, especially in playoff games, ensures a victor is indisputable. It's in the style of how overtime differs between the NFL and the NCAA that debate lies."

I sat back, impressed. For slightly more than her required five minutes, she eloquently broke down the differences between the systems, the debates involved, and then succinctly and forcefully advocated her position. She never glanced at her notes, never even took them out of her pocket. She just... spoke. It was a masterclass in short persuasive speech.

"The truth is that regardless of the overtime system that is adopted, there will always be a certain advantage of one over the other," she said, coming to her conclusion.

But the truth was, I'd struggled to hear most of what she said, staring almost the entire time at those lush, dark red lips, and remembering what they felt like pressed to mine.

"Chance is part of playing sports," she concluded.

"And until it becomes clear that chance is the only factor involved in victory, the system shouldn't be changed. Thank you."

Her chest rose and fell, and I had to admit to myself that she had never, in all of our class sessions or when I'd seen her around campus, looked sexier than she did during that speech.

Finally, I found a way to break the silence. "Impressive."

I was actually blown away. But I was keeping my shit together.

"One more thing," she said, putting her hands on my desk again, "and this has nothing to do with my speech or my grade. But I had to tell you, because it's been in my head ever since it happened. Every class, every time I see you reminds me of that kiss… and how much I want to kiss you again."

I didn't know what to say. I mean, I *did* know what I wanted to say. I knew what I wanted to do. But I refrained. I had a job and reputation to protect.

Much as I hated to.

After a moment, Jessa nodded sadly, and stood up. "Okay… well, I had to say it, Professor. I'm sorry if I was unprofessional, and—"

"Mason."

She stopped. "Mason?"

"That's my name," I reminded her, standing up and coming around my desk. I reached out, pulling her in close. "If we're going to kiss again, I don't want you calling me Professor. That's goddamn creepy."

Her smile was all the encouragement I needed, and I lifted her chin slightly, cupping her face as I kissed her. She wasn't the only one who'd been thinking of our kiss, and as her lips parted and my tongue touched hers for the first time, a thrill jolted me. I pulled her tighter as our kiss deepened, her hands tight on my back.

"Mason," she whispered, and I pulled back, looking into her eyes. "Before we… well, you made me feel safe the other day. I want to thank you."

"Is this you saying thank you?" I asked softly, and she shook her head. "Then get on your knees."

She smiled and obeyed, the sexiest sight I'd ever seen as she posed, her hands behind her back and her breasts pushed up and out, almost bursting out of her top as she looked up at me with hungry eyes. She waited, sexy and obedient as I undid my belt and dropped my pants, her eyes flickering to the growing bulge in my boxers. She licked her lips, biting the lower one as I freed my erection.

She gulped and I could swear my cock lengthened even further. "Mason… you're… big. Bigger than… others."

"You have lots of experience?" I teased, and she blushed slightly. "No. I don't care, Jessa. And I don't even want to know. You're here, now, with me. Now open those velvety lips. No hands."

I wasn't sure what had come over me, but there was no stopping. Reputation and university position be damned. At that moment in time, I was risking it all. I didn't care.

My lovely girl smiled and opened her mouth, her tongue hanging out lewdly until the tip of my cock touched her pink roughness and she leaned forward, closing her lips around my sensitive head. She was right. I was larger than most men, at least that's what I'd always been told. Even half-hard, I would fill that pretty mouth, and as she sucked I quickly thickened and lengthened to my full size. Her eyes watered, and she moaned around me as she bobbed back and forth, her tongue greedily massaging my shaft.

She pulled off, gasping. "Holy fuck, Mason. Please tell me you're not a two-minute lover?"

I laughed loudly at that, running my hand through her black hair, and pushing it back over her shoulder. "No, darling. I haven't been a two-minute lover since I was about fifteen years old, thank you very much."

What a question.

"Now, you're going to get me halfway to coming. Then, I will lay you back on my desk and ravage your pussy until you cream all over me and I fill you with my cum."

Her breath hitched, her eyes filling with lust. "Well. *That* was a convincing speech."

Guided by my hand, she dove down on my cock, sucking and licking with complete abandon. I guided her with my hand in her hair, but she was totally devoted to my pleasure, plunging herself again and again down my length until I felt...

"My god," I whispered in awe as every inch of my

cock slipped into her mouth and down her throat. Most women in my life were shy about even sucking my cock a little, intimidated by its size. But Jessa Carr not only lavished it… she goddamn devoured it.

I held her there for long seconds, my fingers tightening, my balls churning as her tongue and throat and lips lay unimagined sensations on my cock. Before she could take me further, I pulled her off, the *pop* of my head passing her lips, sexy and coarse.

She looked at me with desire and heat, her lipstick smeared sexily and black eyeliner running down her cheeks. "Mason—"

"Get on my desk and get those jeans off," I growled, stepping back and taking off my shirt.

To assist, I got to work on her combat boots, only to find she had incredibly sexy toes—dainty feet that she used to reach out for me, caressing my shaft and pulling me in towards her butterflied knees and legs. The sight of her long, supple legs leading down to the soft pale pink of her slit had me rock hard and oozing precum before her feet even left my cock to wrap around my back.

"You left the bustier on," I noted as I leaned into her, clasping the back of her neck. "It might get dirty. Filthy even."

"I don't care, Mason," she breathed. "I want it dirty."

I chuckled, pressing myself into her after rolling on a condom. She was tight but wet, slowly giving way to my girth as her mouth opened and I stared into her eyes. When her eyes watered with pain, I paused and pulled back, letting her adjust before pushing deeper. As much as my body wanted to just take her hard, I knew she wasn't ready. She needed to accept me. I wanted her to accept me.

I wanted her to be mine.

We were both trembling by the time my hips met hers and my balls rested against her soft skin. She was lost in the feeling of being filled by me, blindly reaching up to take my hand and entwine our fingers as I leaned in to kiss her before pulling back and thrusting my full length into her with one smooth stroke.

I captured her cry of pleasure in my mouth with our deep kiss, swallowing and savoring it as I stood to keep a hold of her hands. With long, deep strokes we fucked, our bodies moving together and my hips driving all of my cock into her tight, flawless body.

"Mason, yes, yes, yes," she begged, encouraging me. I sped up, watching her eyes and feeling her pussy clench around me. We were going so hard my desk shook as I felt my cock swell and Jessa's ankles locked behind my back.

"Not yet," I growled, holding off my climax by sheer force of will as I took her deep and hard. I didn't want it to end. She was unlike any partner I'd ever had. More beautiful, more responsive... more vulnerable.

"Mason, Mason I... I... I..." she whimpered. Her back arched, her fingernails digging into the back of my hand so hard I could hear something crack as she released, coming on me and pushing me over my own edge.

It was amazing. I couldn't control myself as I hammered her with three quick, savage strokes and exploded, my body spasming and shaking as I flooded her with my seed. The whole time our eyes never broke contact, and when it was over I gathered her into my arms, kissing her tenderly.

"Jessa... I..."

She pressed a finger to my lips, then wrapped her arms around my neck to kiss me again.

I wanted to say so much, and yet I didn't know where to start. It was just as well she stopped me. I didn't know how to say I'd never let myself be unprofessional with a student before. How intense our coupling was. So much more than mere fucking.

I wanted to tell her how I felt, and that I wasn't sure how I could be her professor any longer... because I wanted her as a woman.

But she knew. And somehow I understood. So I kissed her again, our bodies still joined as we basked in the afterglow of our intense coupling. Finally I softened enough to slip out, and she unlocked her ankles from my waist to stand on her own.

"We made a mess," she noted, looking down between her legs, which gleamed with her sex juices. "That's... artistic as fuck," she laughed, removing my condom.

"Artistic?"

She studied the mess, chuckling. "Yeah… I mean, Indy and Griff would…" Her voice trailed off.

I lifted an eyebrow. "Indy and Griff?"

She blushed, nodding. "Um… yeah."

For a moment, I felt anger. Truthfully, I felt like I just got played. "I see."

But it only lasted a moment.

She gulped. "Oh Mason. It's not like that. They are—"

I shook my head, cupping her cheek and kissing her again. "I know. But I do need to have a discussion with my housemates."

It was Jessa's turn to look shocked, as my last words hit her brain. "Housemates? You guys are *housemates?*"

"You were intimate with Jessa Carr."

My words carried across the living room, where Indy and Griff were relaxing, watching something on TV. They both looked at me, their faces revealing everything.

Indy caught on first. "So… were you, Mason."

"What?" Griff asked, looking around. "Wait, guys… what do you mean? Jessa Carr?"

"Griff, it's pretty simple," Indy said, leaning forward and resting his elbows on his knees. "It seems that, in the rather recent past, all three of us have had sex with Miss Jessa Carr. Let me guess Mason… tonight?"

"About an hour ago, in my office," I admitted. "I would have come home sooner, but there was a lot to clean up."

Indy chuckled. "Drawing lab, last Thursday for me. What about you, Griff?"

He swallowed, looking shy or upset or something. Finally, he said, "My office… last Monday."

"Well now, it seems we have an… issue," Indy said with a soft laugh. "Or do we?"

I wasn't pulling any punches. "Guys, I… I like Jessa. As in, I want to see her again and not just for sex."

Griff flinched. "Like hell! We were—"

"Whoa, whoa, whoa!" Indy said, getting in between us. "Fuck guys, both of you chill out! Jesus, two Ph-fuckin'-Ds, and all you're thinking with is your D."

I laughed, taking a step back, and Griff did the same. "Fuck my life," Griff groaned, rubbing at his eye sockets. "That girl is going to be the death of me."

"So you want to date her, too," I said.

Griff nodded. "I took the chairmanship of the art department because I wanted to straighten it out, to make it respected. I never would have risked that except there's something about Jessa that… I mean, we haven't even had a date yet and I'm like 'fuck the art department.' At least she's not in your department, Mason."

Indy raised his finger. "You know, I may have the advantage there, considering I could be out of a job come the end of the semester. Meant to talk to you about that. And if I'm not with the university, well then we can easily see who should be dating the lovely Jessa."

"Fuck me, man!" Griff growled in surprise. "When did this happen, your imminent departure? No wait. Right now we've got a more pressing problem."

"Do we?" Indy said. "Mason, when you realized that Jessa had had sex with Griff and me, how did you feel?"

"For a second or two there, I felt played," I admitted. "Like she came into my office to re-deliver a speech she'd fucked up, which by the way, she nailed on the second try. But one thing led to another as they say. Then afterward she said she kept thinking about our kiss of earlier in the week, and… yeah, there was a small part of me that said I just got fucked for a grade."

"To be honest with you, I bet all of us had that same thought to one degree or another," Indy said. "Let me guess, Griff. You had sex with her right about the time she talked with you about the Spring Show?"

"Yeah," Griff said.

"Mine was after she bombed her first modeling session," Indy said. "Griff, did you have sex with her before or after saying you'd get her into the Show?"

"After."

"And I wasn't going to fire her for one bad session," Indy said, tapping his chin. "Gentlemen, we might have an issue… or we might have an *opportunity*."

"What do you mean?" I asked, snapping my fingers when Indy's question became clear. "Cary, Kai, and Leo."

"Huh?" Griff said.

"It's an open secret in the English department. We just don't talk about it much. Last semester, those three guys started… seeing a student," I said. "They're still seeing her. At the same time. In a relationship."

"Jesus," Griff exclaimed, shaking his head. "Is that… allowed?"

"She's not their student, at least not anymore. And from what I hear, she was a Dean's List student even before she started seeing them, so it's not like it affected her grades any," I said. "I have to admit though I don't know the full scene. Like I said, it's an open secret, not something we discuss in staff meetings over coffee. The guys are discreet, and Birdie's—"

"Birdie?" Indy said, and I nodded. "Birdie… Johnson?"

"Yeah, why?"

Indy stepped back and laughed. "Guess who Jessa Carr's roommate is?"

I blinked, then laughed. "So you're saying… *damn.*"

"Guys, wait," Griff said, sitting back down on the couch. "Indy, are you suggesting that, what, we do like this group and… share Jessa Carr?"

"If she's up for it, why not?" Indy asked. "I mean, when I've got the choice between sharing a woman like Jessa or not having her at all, I know what my choice is. And if she has gone to all three of us… well, I suspect trying to force her to choose only one of us would just end up with all of us lonely and jacking off in the shower."

He had a point. A really good point. I might have

kissed Jessa, but Griff and Indy sampled her bodily delights sooner than I did. But it raised a question. "What if she doesn't want to… you know, be shared?"

"It's her choice, of course. If she's not down with it, then game over. But, fuck it guys. What can we lose by at least seeing if she's up for the idea? Since last Thursday, I've been spanking the monkey nightly, and if she says no… I'll still be spanking the monkey nightly. What about you, Mason?" Indy asked.

"You've got a point. On two conditions. One, we are all crystal clear that none of this affects how we grade or interact with her as teachers. She's got a B in my class because she's earned a B in my class. And two, it's all voluntary. I won't be blackmailed or do any blackmailing or anything like that. Sorry, and a third. We actually date her. I'm not the kind for booty calls," I said.

Well, I'd had plenty of booty calls in my past. But that was not what I was willing to settle for with Jessa.

"I'm down with that. Griff?" Indy said.

Griff sat back, rubbing his jaw. "I've got to think about it. No offense, but I'm not in the position you guys are. I'm the department chairman, for fuck's sake. I want to date the woman. God knows I do. But I gotta think this through."

"Let me ask you this, Griff," I said, sitting down. "Twenty years from now, thirty years from now, are you going to say 'Damn, I wish I'd stuck closer to Wellshire's rules and made my tenure less controversial?'"

Griff didn't answer, but my point was made.

Indy chuckled. "No wonder you teach public speaking."

13

JESSA CARR

Three professors.

And honestly? I didn't feel a damn bit bad about it.

Why did we have sex? I didn't fuck them for grades. I was certain of it.

I had sex with them because… well, I wanted to. All three of them were strong, sexy men. Each of them was different, each of them I felt safe with. And with their being housemates, my mind filled with all sorts of entertaining, sexy scenarios.

Maybe… Birdie was rubbing off on me?

I chuckled to myself as I crossed the quad towards the dorms, slightly sweaty. After my last class, I was feeling good but also wanted a stretch, so I changed clothes and headed for the student activity center. I was no fitness freak, but I knew the basics, and after an hour evenly split between the weight machines and the cardio deck, I headed back to get some work done. I had an idea for a new painting. I felt awesome for the first time, in a long time.

Truth was, since kissing Mason that first time, my creative juices had been strangely on fire. And since I'd had epic sex with three amazing men, it was like someone had turned up the volume to full blast. I was waking up every morning itching to get behind the easel and start work. I was using every technique I'd ever learned, crazy colors I'd never tried, and was happier than ever with my results.

I'd even had to buy several brand new sketchbooks to try and empty my mind before going to bed every night.

"Well now, there you are."

I stopped in my tracks, the sidewalk blocked by none other than Cole, just a few feet outside my dorm. I hadn't seen him since the night of the frat party, thank god. In fact, I'd stupidly imagined he'd perhaps disappeared into thin air.

Wishful thinking.

Seeing him now drove me back to that place of overpowering anger. I clenched my fists until my fingernails dug into my palms, and had to calm the hate in my voice in order to speak.

"Are you lost?" I hissed. "You don't live on this dorm."

Where was Roxy when I needed her?

He took a couple steps, getting closer until he towered over me. His gaze felt dirty, and I wished I was wearing more than the minimum sports bra top and leggings for my workout.

"You're looking good, baby. Is that for me?" he said.

"Fuck off, you pig. I don't do anything for you."

I tried to push past him, but his face clouded, and he grabbed my arm. "Are you stupid? I've got your father's phone number."

I glanced around and found that no one was around—just when I was desperate to have someone close by. Anyone. It didn't matter who. Instead, it was just Cole and me, and he was looking more aggressive by the moment.

I raised my chin. "I've got his number, too. You're not special."

I pulled my arm away and tried to push past him. It didn't work.

"Stop being rude, baby," he said.

I prayed someone would come by because at least I'd have a witness to his crazy. Someone, anyone would be good.

"I'm not being rude. Just straightforward. And I'll repeat. I want nothing to do with you. Ever."

He shrugged. "Well you should."

"Why?" I asked, gritting my teeth and trying not to scream. I would if I had to. I wasn't that desperate to keep my secrets private. But with him between me and my dorm, and the area deserted, I had to keep my options open for my own safety. I had to stay calm.

I quietly reached into my backpack as if I were looking for my keys. But I was really hoping to find some pencils or scissors—anything sharp so I could shank him if things got out of control.

"Why? Because you don't want me calling Ronald. As much as I'm sure he'd love to hear from me," he said.

I scoffed. "Good luck getting him to take your call. He barely takes mine."

"I don't know," Cole mused, tapping his chin thoughtfully. "I think he'd want to know that his daughter is a whore, just like her roommate."

Fuck. I knew Birdie and her men couldn't keep their secret under wraps for long, but so far nobody seemed to really care about it. But my father wasn't like the average Wellshire University student. And I had to protect Birdie, too.

"What do you want, Cole?" I asked, realizing I didn't have a damn thing in my backpack that would serve as a weapon.

Except my keys. I discreetly positioned them between my fingers. Another thing they taught at freshman orientation.

"Pretty simple," he said. "I want what we pretended to have. And more."

How he'd gotten so delusional was beyond me. "You want a relationship with me? And this is how you thought you'd get it? By *blackmail*?"

"Happens all the time," he replied evenly, and I shivered at the sureness of his voice. "And yes, Jessa. I want a relationship. With all the perks, of course."

The perks... my stomach flipped, and I suddenly

had a very bad taste in my mouth. "I don't see that happening, Cole. Ever."

He dropped his hands, giving me a good guy smile, which made him look even creepier. "Well, you should. I'm not that bad looking, I've got good connections. I'm smart, I'll be able to take care of you and our family. I'm actually pretty funny, you have to admit. And I'm loyal, Jessa. You and I get together, and that's it. You could drop me in the middle of a porn film and I wouldn't even get a hard on if you weren't there."

Okay... That last one was weird. Disturbingly so.

"Yeah, I didn't hear a single selling point. The answer is no. It will always be no. I don't know how many other ways I can say it."

He sneered, his face going from smug to downright repulsive. "Well, how about this for a selling point—I could ruin your life."

Annnnnd, we were to the crux of the whole fucking thing.

I shook my head slowly, wished there was a way I could tear him to shreds with my bare hands. "You'd do that? You'd hurt me, or settle for an unwilling girl-friend? What kind of man does that?"

"Kings, for one. Industry leaders, billionaires. Very fine people, all of them. And I'd want more than just a girlfriend, Jessa. After we graduate we'll get married. We'll have no debt because our parents paid for our educations. It'd be the first step towards the perfect life. In time you'd come to understand why we should be together."

Inside, I shivered. There was no getting through to the guy.

I decided on a different tactic. There was really no choice. "Look, Cole... maybe you're right, okay?" I said, playing for time and safety. "Give me a few more days to think about it?"

He pursed his lips, and for a moment I thought he was going to close the distance between us, and do something terrible. With my keys between my fingers, I clenched my fist, ready to strike if I had to.

"Fine," he said, and I let out a breath. "This Saturday night, I'll come by at six to pick you up. You'll dress like a lady, not... what you normally wear. We'll go out for dinner, and afterwards we'll go to the next step. Oh, and go commando."

"I thought you wanted a lady?"

He shrugged. "Lady in the streets, whore between the sheets. Understood? See you Saturday, baby."

He took off toward his own dorm, and I ran to the door of mine. After a moment of terrified fumbling with my keys, I pushed inside and slammed the door behind me. Then, I ran to my room and locked myself in, collapsing to the floor and sobbing. Fear and panic shook me to my very core, and I cried, my breath hitching until a cramp in my side stopped me.

I'd never been so scared. I staggered to my feet and got my phone, trying to call Birdie and Roxy. "Come on someone be there, please..."

But no one answered. I knew what that meant. Birdie was with her guys, and Roxy was working. I checked the time and saw it was after six o'clock. Birdie was probably having dinner but Roxy should be available soon. I texted her to come over as soon as she could.

The next instant, I was crying again, angry at myself. I'd gotten myself into this predicament. There was no one else to blame.

I stared at my phone, willing someone to call. I needed them.

I sure as hell couldn't talk to my parents, they'd bought into Cole's nice guy façade.

No, I needed to talk to someone who would understand. I sat for a long time trying to think about who I could go to. When the answer came, it was one of those moments where the revelation is both profound, elegant, and amazingly simple. I nearly slapped myself in the forehead, it was such a moment.

Two minutes later I went running out of the dorm. I wasn't sure where I was going. I honestly had no idea. I just knew that everything in my life was fucked up… and I had only one path forward.

Perhaps it was only by chance that thunder struck as soon as I emerged outside, and that a light rain began to fall.

Or perhaps the gods had a sense of irony.

14

GRIFF LEDGER

ONE NIGHT A WEEK, all three of us guys were free at the same time. Nobody had late labs, programs, staff meetings, or regular social activities. It was the one night a week that Indy, Mason, and I could just hang out.

One of us would pick up some steaks, another a nice bottle or two of wine, and the other would act as chef. It was such an ingrained part of our ritual that I believed it was one of the main reasons our house sharing worked so well.

That night was different, though. After the revelation that we'd each slept with Jessa Carr, and Indy's suggestion that we approach her about a 'sharing' arrangement, the tension in the house was real. We each had things we needed to think through.

That's why I suggested changing our dinner from the house to a nearby local steakhouse. A change of venue might help clear the air. At least that's what I was hoping.

Instead, as we nursed our glasses of wine, Indy and I were pretty much silent. Mason was simply late.

"What time is it?" Indy asked.

"Seven… fourteen," I replied, checking my phone. No messages from Mason. "You want to wait? Or order?"

"Give him another five minutes. After that, fuck it. I need some protein."

There was actually a minute left on Indy's deadline when Mason finally arrived, and we immediately ordered our meals. Even after that though, it was still quiet, the three of us just sort of looking around at everything but each other.

Finally, I decided to break the ice. "Doggy style."

"What?" Indy asked, his head jerking towards me.

"Doggy style," I said, taking a deep breath. "That's how Jessa and I… coupled. Doggy style over my desk."

"Nice," Indy replied, a smile spreading across his face. "She rode me like a cowboy right there in the drawing lab. We were on a rickety stool behind the dressing screen. I'll never look at that studio the same way again. What about you, Mason?"

"In my office," he admitted. "On my desk after she blew me."

He stared at his wine like he was back there that day, his eyes heavy-lidded, his smile lascivious.

"She took that whole hog you've got?" Indy asked, impressed.

When I gave him a look, he laughed. "And how would you know the size of Mason's penis?" I asked.

He rolled his eyes. "Dude, remember back in October, his water heater was on the fritz? He used our bathrooms?"

"Yeah…"

"Well, our friend here was walking around the house in his birthday suit."

Mason chuckled. "Dude. Didn't know you had a thing for me."

Indy laughed.

"Next time, I'll wear clothes, since you care so much," Mason added.

"Anyway," Indy continued, "Jessa's had another modeling session, and she did way better. She held her pose beautifully. Of course, I wanted to rip the drape cloth right off her and fuck her into oblivion even as the rest of the class watched. Seriously. I was dying the whole class."

I nodded. "Know what you mean. She stopped by my office, bringing me what she wants to use for the Spring Show. It's sensual, seductive… I nearly asked if we could add a little glaze to it ourselves. At least she snuck me a kiss before she left."

Mason chuckled. "At least you don't have to try and teach in front of her two or three times a week. So how's her piece… is it good enough?"

I scoffed. "One of the finest student I've seen in my time at Wellshire. Will it win? I don't know. I don't get to judge it, thank god."

"I hope she gets it," Indy said quietly. "The scholarship. Has she told you about it?" he asked Mason.

"No. What about it?"

"Seems her parents don't want her studying art. They'd rather she focus on her MRS degree," I said, shaking my head. "Mr. and Mrs. Carr seem to have been willing to foot the bill for their daughter's education as long as she was… dangling her bait, so it seems. But without any prospects, and the fact that she's studying art, they feel like they're wasting their money."

I hated to hear that. It was wrong on so many levels.

"So *that's* what that guy was about," Mason said. "She'd probably gotten him to play a role, try to distract her folks. A fake date."

"I wouldn't doubt it. You said she was dressed down from her normal style," Indy said. "If she were wearing what she was when I spotted her walking her parents around campus, then I'd guess she was smokescreening them."

I thought about it. "So what do we do?"

"We're going to need to talk to her," I said honestly. "How do you want to do it?"

We discussed the idea over the rest of dinner. While we still weren't sure just how we wanted to proceed, we could agree on a few things. One, Jessa was unlike any undergrad any of us had ever met. She had maturity, even if it needed to be tempered with experience. But her work, her outlook on life?

We had nothing but respect for her on that.

Second, we knew that whatever relationships developed, we'd have to be careful. With her being an art major, Indy and I would have to be on eggshells around her, at least when it came to her academic work. Truth was, I couldn't review even a single piece of work she turned in. I was already bending the rules enough putting her in the Spring Show.

But all three of us were willing to take the risk.

"I have a question, and this is sort of related," Indy said as we enjoyed our desserts. "What if she only wants one of us, or two? Not all three?"

"We might be jumping the gun here," Mason said. "Put it this way. If she doesn't want me, I'll accept it. Definitely won't like it, but I'll accept it."

"Same here. Indy?" I asked, looking at him.

He tapped his spoon on the table for a moment. "If that's the case for me, I think I'll quit my job, become a part time maintenance man, drink a lot of Coors, and maybe open a karate dojo."

"This isn't *Cobra Kai*," I laughed, and Indy grinned. But I was glad he was on board.

After dessert, Indy and I drove back to the house. Mason, needing to gas up his car, said he'd be a few minutes behind. Driving was slow since the afternoon clouds had turned into a pretty intense rainstorm, and my wipers beat a dance on the windshield as we drove.

"Hey, your roof doesn't leak, does it?" Indy asked, craning his neck to look at the darkening sky. "Or are we going to be backstroking out of bed?"

"If I remember correctly, the main house had a brand new roof three years ago... not sure about Mason's place. He can crash on the couch if need be."

We got back to the house, but as soon as I pulled up in the driveway, I saw something was off. There was someone sitting on the porch, and as Indy and I got out, we saw who it was.

"Jessa?"

She looked like a drowned puppy. Her normally sleek, beautiful hair hung around her face in strings, her creamy skin deathly white as she shivered in a windbreaker and tights. "Griff! Indy! I... I didn't know...."

"Shhh," Indy said, mounting the steps. Lights hit us again and I saw that Mason had rejoined us. "Come on, let's get inside. You look like you're freezing."

"T... t... took me t... time to f... f... find your house," she said, her teeth chattering. "I didn't know..."

"That's okay," I said, quickly unlocking my door and opening it. I turned on the heat while Indy helped Jessa inside, Mason closing the door behind us as soon as he could. I turned, seeing that Jessa didn't want to come further in. "What is it?"

"I'm... wet," she said. "I'll ruin your carpet."

"Fuck the carpet!" Mason growled, and I had to agree with him. "Come on, get that wet stuff off. I'll go get you a towel."

"He's right," Indy said. "And I just happen to have a fluffy cotton robe in my room. It'll be a bag on you, but you can wear it while we put your stuff in the dryer."

"Good idea, Indy," I said, looking worriedly at Jessa. She normally wore dark colored lipstick, but now her lips were tinged in blue, she was so cold. "And I'll get some tea on. Jessa, whatever it is that brought you here… you're safe."

Whatever it was that was troubling her, my words were what she needed, because she promptly began to fall apart, her lips trembling before the tears started. Indy hugged her, and I joined in for a moment before going off on my mission.

Whatever broke Jessa… was about to be broken by me.

15

JESSA CARR

THE WARM AIR from central heating instantly warmed me, along with Indy's robe. Griff's Earl Grey tea was a godsend, and Mason found a comb for my hair.

But it still felt awkward, sitting on Griff's sofa surrounded by all three men. Sure, I knew after Mason's comment that they lived in the same house, or something like that. Maybe that was why I hadn't approached them before.

Each one of them was a wonderful man. And maybe all three were good housemates, possibly even friends.

Would my presence turn them into bitter enemies?

"How did you find my place?" Griff asked as he brought me my second cup of tea.

They'd given me time to warm up, protectively focused on my health and safety. Even Griff's choice of teacup, a double insulated travel mug with a handle that was barely warm on the outside so as not to burn my hands, showed that he cared.

And I finally felt human again.

I sighed. "I wandered for a long time before using my phone for the intranet," I said, referring to the Wellshire student network. It was true, I'd rushed around like a chicken with my head cut off for nearly an hour in the rain before I thought to just look him up. "I didn't realize you'd be out for the night."

"But my address isn't on there," Griff said.

"No… but your fans are," I said simply, and Griff looked shocked. "You didn't know? You're considered one of the hot profs. I normally stay off those comment boards, but the art department's board was very helpful."

"And how many fans do I have?" Indy jokes, helping me smile. "Please tell me it's more than Professor Starched White Shirt here."

"I happen to like starched white shirts," I chided, and Indy laughed. "But yes, you're mentioned a lot too, Indy." I looked at Griff, who looked like he was having a heart attack. "Griff? You okay?"

"I just… I guess… head's about to explode," he said. "Do I want to know more?"

"Well, that's how I found your address. I'm surprised no one else has ever shown up on your doorstep. Anyway, how did you three come to live together?" I asked. "Some of the comments wondered if you three were… well, I know you're not, so take that for what it's worth."

"It's my house, but Indy and I go way back," Griff said. "Mason rents the in-law unit."

"Ah." I sipped my tea. "So I guess you three have been… talking?"

"We've compared notes," Griff conceded. "How about I sum it up for us? Get it out in the open?"

I gulped and nodded, not sure what they were going to throw my way.

"You've been with all three of us. Me first, then Indy, then Mason. And you're pressing hard on the Spring Show because your parents are apparently wanting you to get married instead of educated. You need the scholarship." He chuckled, shaking his head.

"And you set up a fake boyfriend at one point," Mason added. "The one you kicked?"

"Yeah… Cole," I said. "Which is why I came tonight. I'm screwed."

"How so?"

I took a deep breath, steadying myself. "My parents are conservative, as you'd guess. How I turned out the way I have is a mystery, honestly. If they knew that I was posing for Indy's class, that I was faking a boyfriend… that I was having sex with three professors? They'd lose their shit. Just to top it off, I have the worst fucking luck in the world in picking fake boyfriends. I could have had my choice of a dozen guys who'd have agreed, done the deal and kept their mouth shut for my hundred dollar payment. Instead, I chose Cole. Who just threatened to ruin my life if I don't agree to date him. And do other stuff."

"Holy shit," Indy said, and I nodded. "Does dating mean what I think it does?"

"With full benefits," I admitted, fending off the nausea that thinking about him caused me.

I shivered, the horror of it all sweeping through me, and Griff put an arm around my shoulders. "Jessa, you don't have to say any more if you don't want."

I wiped at my face, shaking my head. "I need to. It's like… it's like I've got this festering ugliness in my head and I need to just get it out."

"You always have had a good mind for picking effective language," Mason said.

"Thank you," I said, taking a deep breath. "He has this whole plan in his head. He'll intern with my father over the summer, where we can become a real couple in his mind. Then we'll stay in school for the next two years, finish up our degrees, get married… the whole sitcom lifestyle. Except he wants me to be his Stepford wife."

The reality hit me again and the world swam in tears. I thought I was so strong, so tough, but I crumbled like an overbaked cookie as the enormity of my mess came crashing in on me. My shoulders shook, and despair washed over me for the umpteenth time.

Until I felt a pair of arms embrace me, warm and strong. And then another pair, and then a third pair, holding me safe and warm.

"Shhh, it'll be okay, Jessa," Mason said quietly in my ear, rubbing my shoulder. "I happen to have Cole in class tomorrow. I can fuck with his life too, so don't even worry."

"We're here for you," Indy said. "Tell us. What do you need?"

"I need," I said after a moment, "to make love. Not fuck, but… something else."

I looked around at the guys, who all looked back at me in a bit of surprise and hunger. It was pure hunger though, nothing corrupt or vile about it. Instead, they were all committed to me, and that commitment left me feeling… whole again.

"Who would you like?" Griff asked, and I smiled, reaching down to cup him through his pants.

"You," I said, before turning and cupping Indy. "And you." I reached out with my foot, feeling Mason and smiling more. "And you."

"And here I thought we'd be in charge," Mason said, making me smile.

"Sometimes," I assure them. "But as you already know, I'm an opinionated bitch who likes to be heard."

"And how would you like to be heard then?" Griff asked. "Any way you want."

First, of course, we had to get naked. I leaned in to whisper in Griff's ear and he gave me a surprised look but nodded. Without saying anything to Indy or Mason, he got up and left the room, heading toward the back of the house.

"Where's he… I'm sure he'll be back," Indy said, turning his attention to me. "What would you like, Jessa?"

"Kiss me."

Indy pulled me close, our bodies pressing together

as his lips found mine. He had a bit of scruff on his jawline, roughness that added to the sensation as our kiss deepened. He lifted me up, laying me on the big sofa before joining me, his body warm and strong.

And hard. Feeling his cock pressing against my thigh, I knew I had what I wanted.

He kissed down my body, his lips quick and soft, stroking my skin until he found my nipples. "You know how hard these make me?" he teased, stroking my right nipple with his thumb. "I can barely believe they're real."

"They sure are," I said, moaning as Indy pinched my nipple while his teeth captured the other one. His hands stroked down my body, everything lighting on fire as Indy used his hand and mouth together to bring me pure pleasure.

Through slitted eyes I turned my head to see Mason standing there, his cock growing longer and thicker as he took himself in hand, stroking slowly. "Don't worry, this is all for you," Mason assured me as Indy kissed lower. His mouth found my pussy and the world swam. He was unbelievable, and as he feasted on my body I couldn't believe the sensations rushing through me.

I felt a presence near me and I turned my head, opening my mouth for Mason. He was so big my jaw ached as he invaded me, all man and entirely delicious.

"So fucking hot," Indy said before going back down on me, his tongue a dervish on my clit. I melted, moaning around Mason's shaft as Indy made my body quiver. I shook, my stomach clenching as an orgasm rocked me. But Indy wasn't done. His mouth clamped on my pussy lips, soul kissing me. I had to let go of Mason as I cried out again and again, my body coursing with release.

"Yes! Oh fuck yes!" I cried, grinding up into Indy's masterful ministrations. I could feel myself gushing, soaking Indy's face and the couch below us. But I didn't care.

It was beautiful.

Finally he pulled away and I sagged, smiling wistfully. "You enjoyed that?" he asked.

"Can I ask you two to wait for your turns, though? I... I want to give something to Griff."

Griff, who'd returned quietly, stepped forward. "Jessa, are you sure?"

I nodded, smiling lazily. "I am. Completely."

Griff nodded and helped me to the floor. I got to my knees, presenting myself to him as I felt his fingers run over my ass... and then in between my cheeks. The first touch of the lubricant was cool, not cold, but a different kind of sensation as Griff slowly massaged my virgin hole.

Mason knelt down next to me, taking my hand as Griff slipped a finger into me, and I could feel my body resist at first. Mason leaned down, whispering in my ear, "Relax, Jessa. Just push back, Griff's gentle, and I'm here. You're always safe with us."

"I... I know," I said, whimpering as my ass relaxed a little and Griff slipped in farther. I shivered as new sensations flooded my body, Griff carefully massaging and stretching my ass with one hand while using the fingers on his other hand to stroke my pussy and clit.

Mason held me still as I felt Griff withdraw, my body already on edge from his touch. I slowly jacked Mason to distract myself, and Indy knelt down too, making me smile while Griff lined himself up.

"Push back," Griff said quietly and I did, whimpering as I felt him stretch me... and slip inside.

It was... fullness. I'd joked with Birdie and Roxy about giving up the ass. They'd expected me to be the girl who'd done it all. But I hadn't. Assplay was something I'd always been curious about. But that was the extent of it. But as Griff slid his slick, long cock up my ass, I was in a new world. My body was on fire in the best of ways, my spine crackling with little explosions as he slid deeper and deeper.

"You feel so good in my ass, Griff," I grunted as Griff bottomed out in me. "I fucking love it, Griff."

"You're perfect," he assured me as he pulled back. My hands sped up on Mason and Indy's cocks as Griff thrust into me again, and I knew that I was hooked.

Give me three cocks at a time, if it was these three cocks. Griff's thrusts were slow and deep at first, relaxing me and making me feel safe and secure. I was a queen, worshiped by three amazing lovers as Griff held me down, taking over.

I was in paradise. My hands stroked up and down Indy's and Mason's cocks, feeling their steely growth and pulsing arousal as Griff dominated me, his hips slapping against my body as his cock plunged in and out of my bottom.

Mason tensed, his cock swelling in my hands. I grinned, turning to capture his cum. I was too slow, the first shot splattering across my face before the rest went into my mouth. I sucked him hungrily, moaning as Griff sped up, pounding my ass.

"Yes, yes… god I want it," I moaned, pulling off Mason to turn to Indy. "Fuck my ass Griff, come in me…"

Indy thrust in, plugging my mouth, and I gave myself over. Griff and Indy took me from in front and behind, with Indy's hands on my head while Griff gripped my waist.

Griff swelled, his thrusts faster and harder as Indy fucked my face until my nose was pressed against the curly hairs at the base of his dick. I moaned around him as Griff panted, grunting, "I'm gonna come."

"Mmmmmph! Mmmmm!" I tried to reply, telling Griff to give me all of his desire as I trembled on edge myself. Of course my mouth was full of Indy's cock, so he got to feel my orgasm in a whole different way when Griff slammed hard into me one last time, his cock spurting deep inside me as I came again. Moments later Indy threw his head back and came, flooding my mouth with his sweet-salty cream.

I was utterly, completely satisfied… and safe. I sagged to the carpet, where Griff followed me, Indy sandwiching me while Mason knelt above me, stroking my hair and cradling my head.

"You guys…" I started, emotion catching and stopping my words for a moment. "Thank you."

"Thank *you*," Mason said, brushing my hair back. "So… what now?"

I thought for a moment, and sighed happily. "Now, if you don't mind, Mason, I think I need a shower. Care to join me?"

Mason laughed softly. "We can't fit four people in the showers here."

"This won't be the only shower I take here. Griff, Indy, is that okay, if Mason takes me in the shower?"

"Takes a shower with you, or takes you in the shower?" Indy teased before kissing my lips. "Either way, I'm okay with it."

I was more than okay with it, too.

16

INDY DAWSON

"How are you feeling?"

We sat at the kitchen table, eating a late breakfast of pancakes prepared by the lovely Jessa.

On top of everything else, the woman could cook.

I was ready to marry her right there.

Mason had already left for campus, taking Jessa back to the dorms since his parking lot was the closest, leaving Griff and me to eat alone.

"What do you mean, how am I feeling?" I asked.

"You know, after last night?" Griff asked, helping himself to another pancake.

"Well, let's see... once I got past my bruised ego since Mason's hung like a fucking racehorse," I said, making him double over in laughter, "I was fine. Hey. I'm confident in my manhood."

"Jessa didn't seem to mind your performance. She wasn't exactly complaining, as I remember it. So I think you're okay there," he said.

"She's so hot. When she loses her shit, well... I don't think I've ever seen anything like it. But hey, that was hot as fuck the way you took her ass. Most dudes would have had her crying in pain, not moaning in orgasm. I don't think she'd ever taken it that way."

Griff looked down at his plate, shaking his head in disbelief. "How weird is this, that we're talking about having sex with the same girl at the same time, comparing notes and all?"

I shrugged. "Beats focusing on what I've got coming up today. I figure the less I think about it, the less I'll be tempted to beat the shit out of that psycho Cole, who's been tormenting Jessa."

"What do you have planned for him?"

"Nothing physical if I can help it," I assured him. "As I understand it, he needs to pass my Intro to Art class."

"To keep the scholarships he's got, right?" Griff asked. "Is he passing?"

"Could go either way," I said noncommittally. It wasn't too much of a stretch, really. Cole was definitely half-assing it as someone who took Intro because he thought it'd be an easy elective. "He doesn't put much effort in."

"I see."

I could see the ambivalence Griff was feeling. He was a true academic, and the idea of resorting to *teaching someone a lesson* didn't feel good.

"Is there any potential blowback I should be aware of?" I asked.

To be honest, even if there were, I wasn't sure I cared.

"Well," Griff said, "you're a visiting scholar whose position is about to end. You're probably safe. Unless, you know, you want to stay at the university. Get another job or something. If that's the case, then teaching Cole a lesson is something you'd better do very discreetly."

"Good to know losing my job is helpful for something."

We left for campus, where I threw myself into a day of teaching. I might not have been a true professor, but I did want to teach all my students everything I could. Most of them, especially the art majors, were truly committed to learning. Even the non-art majors had the occasional diamond in the rough.

It wasn't until my last class of the day that I had to deal with Cole. I struggled to get through the lecture, forcing myself to remain professional as I led everyone through a review of cubism. After handing out assignments, I dismissed the class early, asking Cole to wait for a moment afterward.

After class cleared out and we were alone, I let him cool his heels for a bit. He shifted on his feet, glancing around the room, looking everywhere except at me.

"Cole, I was doing a review of everyone's work. You've got a problem. A failing problem," I said, keeping my voice even and maybe a bit cold. It did what I wanted, which was throw him further off balance than he already was.

He scowled. "Are you serious? Then what can I do to raise my grade?" he asked. "I need to keep my grades up for my scholarship."

He was walking into my web, just as I'd hoped.

I stared at his worried face, wishing I could rearrange his nose. "Well, as a matter of fact, I do have an idea for you. Because, you know, with art, as in life, character counts."

"Wh… what do you mean?"

Of course he had no freaking idea what that meant. Because he had no character.

"This is what I mean, Cole. I hope you'll listen very carefully, because this is very important."

I paused for a moment, watching the trickle of sweat run down the side of his face.

"Cole, I know you've been harassing another student. It's time for you to stop."

Confusion crossed his face, which was no real surprise. He was an obvious idiot.

I continued. "See Cole, twenty percent of your grade depends on my teacher evaluation. Currently, you're more or less middle of the road. How you act in the next few weeks will have a big impact on this twenty percent, which you need to score highly on to get a decent grade out of the class."

"Wh… what do you mean, harassing? I'm… not harassing anyone," he stumbled.

"Don't play dumb. It's not going to help you, and will only further irritate me." I took a step closer to him and put my finger in his face.

"Leave... Jessa Carr... alone," I said in a quiet voice.

He took a step back as realization washed over him, followed by a nasty little smirk.

My jaw twitched. It was all I could do to keep my hands of the fucker. If I punched him, I'd go to jail and that wouldn't help anyone.

"Here's the deal, Cole. You don't speak to her, you don't go to her dorm, you don't have contact with her or anyone she knows. She gets in your line at the dining hall, you either go take a piss break or serve her without making eye contact. You see her walking to class, you head in the other direction. You so much as smell her perfume or hear her voice, you disappear. You do this, you get a twenty percent bump to your grade, and skate out with a solid B. You don't get your shit together, well, you'll enjoy the impact of a failing grade on your GPA. We'll see what that does to your scholarship. And one more thing. I am not fucking kidding, not even a little."

In an instant, he transformed right before me. One minute, he was a worried but normal college kid, maybe a little dumb-looking with all that bafflement on his face. The next, he darkened, storm clouds rising in his eyes, fists clenched by his side.

Okay. *This* was how it was going to be.

"Jessa, huh?" he growled, his voice now raspy and aggressive. "Is that little slut tempting you now?"

"Are you fucking kidding me—" I started, but my words were cut off. Cole kicked the nearest chair, sending it skittering across the floor before it tipped over on an uneven tile. I jumped to my feet, ready to beat his ass if I had to.

"So," he said, brandishing his book like an awkward weapon. "You'll fail me? We'll see about that then, won't we, Professor Dawson. Of course, there's something you forget." He tapped his temple with a finger.

He thought he was making himself look smart..

I had to try not to laugh.

"What's that Cole?"

"This semester's going to end… and then what are you going to do? You won't be able to stop me if I decide to teach her my own lesson or two. You won't be around."

Before I could respond, he left, kicking the classroom door open as he made his departure. Part of me wanted to go after him, grab him by the neck of his preppy polo shirt, and drag him to the ground.

Uncertain as to whether I'd helped or hurt the situation, I went home, barely containing my rage. But I had a welcome boost to my troubled mood when I found Jessa in the kitchen waiting for me, a smile on her face.

"You are the best thing I've seen all day," I said as she came over, wrapped her arms around my neck, and gave me a big kiss. "And you're the best thing I've tasted."

"I don't know, lunch was pretty tasty," she teased before giving me another kiss. That one went deeper, and when I reached down to cup the curve of her ass, she moaned into my mouth, leaving me aching hard in seconds. "Mmm… Indy, you're tempting me, but I can't right now."

"Can't?" I asked, and she nodded. "Everything okay?"

"More than okay," she said, pulling back and giving me a big smile. "It's why I'm here. I got formal notification that... I got into the Spring Show!"

"That's awesome!" I grabbed her and twirled her until she screamed for me to put her down.

"It is, buuuut… there's something I wanted to talk with you guys about," she said. "I was gonna wait for the others to get home, but I guess I can tell you since you're here. I re-read the rules, and an entrant is allowed to replace their piece with a new one if they want."

"Right. They want the artist to be excited about what they're showing," I said. "So you're thinking of doing something new?"

"I am… I mean, I can do it and still go with my original if it doesn't work," she explained, and I had to agree. "I know it will be great, though. The way I'm feeling because of you three guys is so magical. I'm totally inspired. Anyway, I wanted to tell you in person that you all have planted the seeds for the crazy creative energy I'm feeling. It kind of scares me, the enormity of it, but I'm taking it one step at a time."

"Good."

She tilted her head, smiling a little. "Good?"

"Yes, good," I repeated. "Jessa, great art should scare the hell out of you. Did you know that Michelangelo was practically paralyzed with fear by the enormity of what he was attempting at the Sistine Chapel? Great art should leave you trembling inside as you approach it, knowing that what you're attempting is going to be hard. If it were easy, everyone would be doing it."

She took a deep breath, and nodded. "I just want to make you guys proud."

"Fuck that," I said, coming closer and putting my hands on her shoulders. "I am, and will always be, proud of you. Regardless of what you do in the Spring Show. The only person you need to worry about with this piece is the badass sexy bitch that you see in the mirror every morning."

"And if I need to have time to myself?" she asked nervously. "You know, to focus? To channel these energies inside me? I just feel like if I'm around you guys, I'm going to be so tempted to unleash this feeling in a totally different way."

"In other words, you don't want to fuck the art out of you," I joked, and she laughed. "It's okay, we're not critics, we don't need the flowery language, Jessa. And I get it. I mean, I'll be spanking it like a freak after every modeling session you do, but I get it. And I support you."

"I promise that afterward, I'm going to show you the full depth of my appreciation," Jessa promised, and I chuckled.

"The sex is good, I won't lie," I said. "But Jessa, I want more than your body. Catch my drift? So do what you need to… I'll be here. Just do me one favor."

"What's that?"

"Hang out here until Griff and Mason get back from school. I want you to hear directly from them that they feel the same way I do," I said. "So that when you're off painting and all that, you know without a single doubt how much support you've got."

Jessa's smile was reward enough for any sacrifice we guys had to temporarily make.

Temporary being the key word.

17

JESSA CARR

THE MAIN AUDITORIUM in Wellshire Hall was packed, if not with fans, at least with art. There were a dozen pieces in the competition, and the committee had also reserved spaces for graduating students to display their favorite work even if they weren't in the actual show.

The crowd was big. I'd counted over two hundred different people in the time I'd been standing by my piece, and I was sure more were filtering in and out since I was released after the judges came by and spoke with me about it. I also got to talk to Birdie and Roxy, giving them a fuller story on the painting.

I'd titled it *Fulfillment,* and if the initial piece I'd applied with was as sensual as Griff had said, this was sensual times four... hundred. I'd poured myself into this project harder than I ever had before, painting in the lab until security chased me out each night, only to be right back at it the next morning.

Fulfillment represented my blood, sweat, tears... and

newfound sexuality. It was a natural thing to create, considering how horny I was from painting and the posing sessions for Indy's class. I know he was aroused by the time I finished my fifty minutes each time, and the idea of his stroking his cock while thinking of me had me dripping with almost no effort.

Now that I was done with the judges and free to roam, I saw the guys hanging out together, and made my way over, doing my best to appear calm and professional.

They tried to remain professional, as well.

"Jessa, how'd it go?" Indy asked.

"I feel good," I told him, looking him up and down. "So you *can* dress up, I see."

He laughed, tugging on the lapels of his sport coat. He wasn't fully dressed up, still wearing a T-shirt underneath. But it was a clean, stylish shirt, not like his usual faded concert Ts, and he was rocking a very cool dude vibe. He adjusted his glasses and pushed his hair behind his ears. "I've been known to clean up from time to time. Hey, did you see my piece?"

"I did," I said, looking back over my shoulder. Indy had slipped one of his painting in for the 'scholar showcase,' and it was mind-blowing. The way he used color and shape to emphasize the feeling he was going for brought tears to my eyes. "When did you find time to do it?" I asked.

"I have to admit it's from last semester," he said with a chuckle. "I tried doing a piece over the past few weeks, but it was a little too… voluptuous, I would say."

"Ah… with black hair?" I asked, and he shrugged. It warmed me, and I looked around. "Hey guys, can we talk privately?"

The four of us slipped to the back of the auditorium near the fire exit, a shadowy area that wasn't part of the show but was instead being used as storage for the stuff that had to be moved out of the way for the exhibit. As soon as we were alone, I turned to them. "I've missed you all. A lot"

Mason smiled, taking my hand. "We've missed you too. At least Indy and I got to see you in class."

"I don't know if that was easier or harder," I said, blushing. "You were sexy as fuck in class this past week."

"Gotta admit I was a little inspired."

"Jessa, regardless of what the judges say," Griff said, taking my other hand, "we're all proud of you. That piece was absolutely stellar. Better than anything I've ever done."

"Don't say that," I teased, stepping closer and putting my arms around his neck. "I couldn't have done it without you, Griff. Any of you. Thank you for all the love and support over the past few weeks."

It was true. We might not have been having sex, or spending nights together, but there were little ways the guys made sure I was taken care of. Whether it was Cole staying out of my hair, or the packet of high quality brushes that came in my mailbox, or just the 'anonymous' e-card of encouragement.

"We're here for you no matter what, Jessa," Griff

said, and the other guys nodded. I smiled and stood on tiptoe, kissing Griff despite the fact we were in the auditorium. Indy was next, and then Mason. Each one was short but sweet, with a promise of what was to come the rest of the weekend.

I wanted them. To love, to have, to share. I wanted to explore their souls in ways that we hadn't had the opportunity to yet, and the chance to ignite torrid flames of passion that would threaten to torch Griff's home to the ground if we weren't careful.

I wanted to explore the limits of my sexuality with these men... and I wanted it soon.

We were so distracted by our hasty reunion and the delayed, desired kisses that none of us noticed anything until I turned around to see my father and mother standing there, aghast. In the background I saw Cole disappear into the crowd, and knew what had happened.

I'd just been set up.

"Jessa!" Mom exclaimed, turning pasty. "Is this... is this what..."

"Didn't I raise you better than this?" Dad accused, his eyes filled with hurt and anger.

"Mom, Dad, let me explain—"

"Explain nothing, young lady!" Mom hissed, looking around as if the crowd was going to come circle like buzzards. "You... you're acting like—"

"Meredith dear," Dad said, sniffing, "we should hold ourselves to a higher standard and not engage with these... people."

My mouth fell open as my emotions boomeranged between shame, anger, humiliation, and guilt.

"Mr. and Mrs. Carr, if you would—" Mason started, but Dad leveled him with a finger, pointed straight at his face.

"You say one more word and you'll be picking your teeth up off the floor," Dad said.

I guessed the whole higher standard thing was abandoned pretty quickly. Dad dropped his hand and looked at me. "I hope these men are supporting you… because I'm done with you. Come on, Meredith."

I felt nailed to the floor as Dad and Mom hurried off. Just beyond them, I saw Cole again, smirking as he shrugged, holding his hands out as if saying *what did I do?* He turned and sauntered off, his hands in his pockets, not a care in the world.

I was left with Griff, Indy, and Mason, who were speechless .

Finally, Griff spoke. "Fuck," he said. "Jessa, I'm sorry, I shouldn't—"

"No," I said, inhaling deeply and pushing back my feelings. "If anyone is to take the blame, it's me. I should have met you guys back at the house or something, not… here."

"No Jessa, the person who should be blamed for this is Cole," Indy growled, clearly pissed. "In fact, I should go let him know that with my foot right up his ass."

"No!" I protested, putting a hand on his arm. "I mean, he caused this, but we can't take that route. We have enough going on without your getting arrested.

Look, I need… I need to think. Do you guys mind if we meet back at the house at say, six p.m. or something?"

"You sure?" Mason asked, and I nodded.

The guys left and I drifted around the rest of the show for another hour, trying to figure out what the hell had just happened in my life, and what I was going to do about it. At least it seemed that nobody had noticed… or perhaps nobody was willing to say anything about it at the show. Eventually, though, I had to get out of there. I walked to Griff's house, where I found the guys waiting for me on the porch.

"How're you feeling, sweetie?" Griff asked.

I shrugged. "Weird. On one hand I'm scared to death, my stomach flip-flopping as my brain keeps jumping from one scenario to the next. Then I try to tell myself that it's not that bad, that it'll work itself out. The next instant I'm despondent again. Griff, have you heard about the show, or the scholarship?"

I knew it was early yet but good news—any sort of good news, was more than welcome at that moment.

Griff shook his head, standing up. "No. It's an outside panel. They'll take anywhere from two hours to two months to get the answer back to the department. As long as they get it in time for the next semester, nobody seems to really care."

I nodded, slumping. "So now what?"

"Now," Mason said, standing up and holding out a hand, "we take you inside and help you forget. At least for a night."

I thought about it for a moment, then nodded

wearily. I wanted them, yes. But my heart was heavy. Still, Mason's hand on mine helped, and as he led me upstairs I knew that, if nothing else, I would have one hell of an endorphin rush to help deal with all my shit.

Griff led the way to his bedroom, where the king sized bed looked huge compared to the narrow dorm room bed I was used to. He knelt at my feet, untying the complicated knots I'd used for my boots that day, carefully loosening the pink laces to free my feet.

Indy stood next to me, fingering the zipper that held my top up. "How do women get zippers like this closed?"

"Roommates mostly," I replied, shivering as he ran a finger down my spine. His touch was mirrored by Mason, who helped him strip off the rest of my upper body clothing while Griff removed my stockings and skirt.

When they were done, I was as naked as the day I was born. The desire in their eyes helped lift my mood, and seeing Indy stiffen in his jeans without even touching me made me smile. "Like what you see?" I teased, the turmoil of earlier in the day slipping away, even if only momentarily.

He reached down, cupping his bulge, and nodded. "Every inch of it."

"I think you're all wearing too many clothes," I noted, sliding onto the bed and laying back. "Join me please?"

Their response lifted my mood even more, as I watched three sexy, beautiful men turn into a tornado of flailing arms, hands tugging at shoestrings, zippers unzipping, and clothing landing on the floor in piles. I watched Griff pull his shirt off so forcefully that a seam ripped and buttons went flying.

But it was worth it because in seconds he climbed onto the bed and into my open arms.

"So lovely," he said before kissing me. His lips were soft at first, sweet and expressive, but we quickly went deep, our tongues twisting and tasting.

We were soon joined on the bed by Indy and Mason, their hands electrifying me as they moved up my legs. Lips followed, and I gasped into Griff's mouth as someone stroked my inner thighs and then my pussy with feathery touches.

Hands caressed me all over and I had no sense of which belonged to whom. All I knew was that these men were lighting my nerves on fire.

"Griff," Indy rumbled from between my legs, "you have to taste this pussy."

"Mmmm, I already have, remember?" Griff said, smiling.

I looked down to see Indy between my legs, swiping his tongue over my puffy, wet lips, leaving me shivering with desire. He looked very happy, like he could do that all night if I wanted, and I ran my hand through his messy hair, urging him deeper.

He was magical. His tongue stroked and nibbled at me in a way I'd never thought possible, darting deep into my folds before teasing my lips, going back for more and then circling my clit.

I was in heaven. My eyelids fluttered, and I let myself be swept away by his attentions. Griff hummed, and I smiled, reaching to take his erection in my hand. "Indy's not the only one who can use his mouth, you know," I told him with a smile.

Griff shifted, and the head of his cock flushed a delicious pink. It was with hungry lips that I turned to taste him, licking him slowly before sucking on the sensitive flare of his erection.

The rhythms of my mouth on Griff and Indy's on mine mirrored each other. Mason, on my other side, shifted and I felt his mouth capture my left nipple, fresh heat blooming in my chest as I devoted myself to sucking Griff.

I tried to draw it out, but it wasn't long before Griff was gripping my head, his fingers tight in my hair as he took over, thrusting in and out of my eager lips as Indy left me shaking and trembling. I came, moaning around a mouthful of Griff's dick, but Indy didn't stop what he was doing between my legs. If anything, his tongue sped up, rushing me towards another climax that promised to be even bigger.

"Fuck Jessa... suck harder. I'm coming baby," Griff grunted just before his cream filled my mouth. I whimpered, sucking up every tasty droplet as Indy guided me through another orgasm.

When Griff pulled out of my mouth, I screamed, nothing moving through my mind but the high of sex and passion devouring me. "Indy... Indy... fuck me before I pass out," I begged. "You then Mason."

My head spun literally as I was flipped over and pulled up onto my knees. Indy sheathed himself, then entered me with one deep stroke. I gasped, my head pulled back as he grabbed my hair and held me still.

It was rough and savage and emotional and... everything I wanted. Indy's hips slapped against my upturned ass, my body limp with exhaustion. Griff helped me, holding my shoulders as Indy grunted and thrust, his cock making lewd sucking sounds as my pussy clung to him, jolted with each deep stroke.

"Jessa!" Indy growled, and a moment later filled me with the warm pulses of his climax. I was so worn out I was ready to collapse, but as soon as Indy was done, I cried out as Mason took his place, stretching me with his big cock.

Mason's strokes were different, not as savage as Indy's but deep and unrelenting. He built me up even as he pressed me to the mattress, holding my waist in his hands as I shivered, so very close to my edge.

I wanted to make it last forever. When they were pleasing me, I could forget... what needed forgetting. None of what happened that day mattered any longer. All that did was the feeling of Mason's hands on my hips, his cock stretching me open, and the feeling of my spine being jolted with each stroke while Griff leaned in for another kiss.

But of course I couldn't fuck forever. I felt myself tightening, squeezing, and milking Mason as a third orgasm came rushing up on me. My hands clenched the bedspread, and with a deep cry I broke apart, shattering. Darkness came rushing up, swallowing me entirely. I embraced it. I knew I was safe, and that in the darkness I could find relief from the pain of the real world.

It wasn't just what I *wanted*—it was also what I *needed*.

18

MASON ACKER

I sat at my desk, trying to control my temper as I stared at the papers in front of me. I had seen Cole, that gutless son of a bitch, crossing campus at lunch looking as happy as a clam. He even high-fived some guy before flirting with a couple girls. It took all my effort not to follow Indy's previous inclination to go after him and teach him a lesson.

Now, three hours later, I was still fuming as I struggled to grade a series of freshman papers. Not that they were doing me any favors. Half the students could barely put together a grammatically correct sentence, while the other half thought that channeling their inner favorite classical author would somehow make their work better.

I wasn't sure who was more tedious, the ones who followed their inner Melville to stretch thin arguments out to fit the required essay length, or the ones who thought Hemingway and his brevity were the epitome of writing.

At least the Hemingway devotees were exactly on word count and no more.

I was about to dive into the next essay when there was a knock on my office door. I looked up to see Jessa standing there, worry clearly lining her face.

"They're ghosting me."

"What?" I asked, standing up. "What do you mean, ghosting you? Who?"

"I've tried calling my parents, e-mailing them, texting them," she said quietly, her shoulders slumping. "Mason, they haven't responded at all, and the last time I tried to call my Dad's cell phone, you know what it did? It rang once, then disconnected. You know what that means, right?"

"He was busy?" I offered helpfully.

But Jessa shook her head.

"Hardly. Dad never swipes me down. Honestly I'm not even sure if he knows *how* to swipe down a call. He's always let it go to voicemail if he can't answer. Mason, he's blocked my number. I have to reach them. I have to."

Part of me wanted to tell her to not waste her time. If her parents were angry, they either needed time to cool off, or they were truly cutting her out of their lives. Reaching out might accomplish nothing but more heartache.

But I knew Jessa well enough to know that she was

going to do what she wanted. She had her own mind, and that was part of what I respected about her. So I set my grading pen down and sat down behind my desk again. "Want some help?"

We got to work, crafting a two page letter that could be used as a persuasive speech. "Read the latest changes," I told Jessa after about an hour, rubbing at my temples. "The paragraph about… us."

"Sure. Here we go. 'Mom, Dad, I know that seeing me kiss three men, all older, was a shock to you. It wasn't the way you grew up, and not what you expected. But you need to know the feelings I have for these men are genuine and not to be diminished. These are good men, solid men, each amazing in his own right.'"

She looked back up at me. "Do you think I should I say anything about the long term, Mason? I mean, I know we haven't really discussed it but I wonder if my parents would be more accepting if they didn't think we were all just on booty calls."

I laughed. "Maybe wait on that. Telling your parents you're looking forward to spending the next decade or five in a foursome relationship with two artists and a comms professor might just blow their minds more than they already are."

"It would have blown *my* parents' minds," Griff said, appearing in my office doorway with Indy right behind him. "It still might, even though they're pretty open minded. But one hurdle at a time."

"What're you two doing? It sounds like you're working on a speech," Indy said, craning his neck to see the computer screen.

After greeting Griff and Indy with a nice smack on the lips, Jessa gave them a rundown of what brought her to my office, and what we'd done so far. I expected Indy to say what I had thought earlier, about how we were wasting time trying to appease Jessa's parents, but instead he grabbed a chair and plopped down. "What about... what about making it a bit more... poetic?"

"Not sure that would work with my dad," Jessa said.

"How did you end up the way you are, then?"

Jessa laughed, and we got back to work. We'd been nearly done, but it was nice to get Griff's and Indy's input.

Jessa read it one more time, nodding to herself. "Well... now what?"

"Now you have to figure out how to deliver it," Griff said. "If you want to mail it, I'd rewrite it on nice stationery, send it registered so they have to sign for it. If you want to deliver it in person or even read it to them... well, I'm up for a road trip this weekend," he said, looking around.

She chuckled, but shook her head. "I'm pretty sure if you showed up, Dad would go get his shotgun."

Jessa closed her laptop. "I'd love to go home with you guys tonight, but I really should brave the dining hall and then get some homework done. I've got this communications professor who drives me hard and long."

She looked right at me. Fuck, she was gorgeous

I smirked. "Thought you liked it that way."

"Oh, I do… in more ways than one," she said, getting up to give me a kiss. "Thank you, Mason. All of you. I… I'll see you tomorrow."

After she left, I could only think about the hitch in her voice. It was too early to give names to our feelings, but I knew what was going on for her. I felt it too.

After she'd gone, I looked at Indy and Griff, both lost in thought.

"Think a letter will do any good?" I asked, even as I knew the answer.

"Not a chance in hell," Indy said, steepling his fingers. "I didn't talk to my parents for years after they realized I was serious about being an artist. Fact is, life ain't a Hallmark movie. Jessa might fix things in the Carr family eventually, but it won't be quick. Or painless."

Griff took a deep breath. "I'm not sure how likely this is, guys, but I just want to put something out there. There's a chance, you know, that she could choose her parents over… us. I hope it won't come to that, but it's a possibility."

I'd considered that, too, but had pushed it out of my mind. Griff's saying it out loud, though, made it all the more real. Her choosing us was anything but a foregone conclusion. It was a fact.

"If it happens, it happens," I said honestly. "There's nothing we can do but support her. I figure it this way. Our feelings for Jessa caused part of the fucking mess she's in right now. Not all of it of course. Her father's a dickhead of the highest caliber based off of what Jessa's told us about him, and what I saw last Saturday sure as hell didn't change that opinion."

"Yup," Griff said.

"So here's what I say. Speaking for myself and maybe you guys as well, what I feel for Jessa… it's authentic. I won't name it without her here, but I can see in your eyes that you probably feel the same way. So we've got to do right by her, and help however she needs us to."

"Totally agree," Indy said quietly. "Speaking of which… I'm going to need to think about my future work options, if nothing comes up here at the university for me, won't I?"

"Probably."

He sighed. "Griff, what about the scholarship? For Jessa? If that little prick Cole said something to her parents, I can guarantee you he'll at least say something to the committee."

"I have no idea where that all stands. I'm not included in the decision making. But you saw her piece, *Fulfillment*. That was good enough to hang in the Met."

"True. Just… fuck, I wish there were more I could do," Indy said. "Seriously."

Griff went silent for a while, thinking. "Indy… maybe there is one way I can help Jessa. But I can't do it alone."

"Yeah?" Indy asked.

"And," Griff said, turning to me. "We might need the help of a good persuasive writer, too. Happen to know one, Mason?"

"I might."

19

JESSA CARR

THE REGISTRAR'S office at Wellshire University wasn't the nicest office on campus, not by a longshot. I didn't know who designed the place, but it didn't fit with the rest of the school. Most of Wellshire's buildings were academic, with dark wood and high ceilings. You could practically smell the higher learning, all testaments to deep pocketed alumni who wanted to leave a permanent impression on the ol' alma mater.

Apparently, though, nobody cared about the registrar's office, or if they did, they were a certified sadist. Because the only thing that the registrar's office could be compared to was the DMV, minus the unintentionally funny traffic safety posters.

"Can I help you?" a bored clerk asked as I stepped forward.

I fished out my phone to show her the e-mail I'd gotten that morning.

She pulled on her glasses and squinted. "Ah. Okay,

that's… Ms. Fulham. Let me see if she's available." She lumbered away from her desk, saying nothing further.

Ms. Fulham was a woman I vaguely remembered from my previous visits. She wasn't anything as glamorous as an academic advisor or guidance counselor. Instead, she was one of the registrar's office workers who dealt with what the school most cared about.

Money.

"Miss Carr, have a seat," Ms. Fulham said after leading me to her cubicle. It was utilitarian, stark really, with faded blue burlap on the thinly insulated soundproof dividers. "Okay, I'm glad you came so quickly, it gives us time to discuss options."

"I don't get it… options?" I said, shaking my head.

Ms. Fulham shifted around in her seat, adjusting her cat's eye glasses before giving me a look. "I'm guessing you weren't told, were you?"

"Told what?" I asked, my heart rate picking up.

Ms. Fulham folded her hands on her desk, giving me an even, professional look. "I'm sorry Miss Carr, but your father notified the university that he was stopping payment on any further tuition for you."

What?

Had someone just kicked me in the guts? Because it sure felt like it.

"He… um… on my god," I mumbled, unable to form a coherent sentence.

My letter. It must have fallen on deaf ears. I thought they understood when they at least let me in the living room to say what I had to say.

How could I be so wrong? And how could they be so cruel?

"Sorry to break this to you, Miss Carr. I see it's caught you by surprise. Perhaps you could have a talk with you father—"

But I cut her off. "What options do I have?" I asked. "I... I still have at least a year of classes left. I have to find a way to stay in school."

My heart was set, of course, on the art scholarship. But I knew not to put all my eggs in one basket. The competition for that money was stiff, and there was no way of knowing whether I'd be the lucky recipient.

Ms. Fulham nodded with a kind smile, which, of course, led to my eyes filling with tears. I'm sure she saw sad sacks like me all the time. "I understand. That's why I'm glad you came in quickly. There's financial aid you can apply for, and we can see what scholarships are out there. The problem is, it takes time to get all this rolling. Let me make you an appointment with one of our counselors. They know every trick in the book, and if you work with them, they'll make sure you get every dime of scholarship or grant money you might qualify for. And if you work a summer job, you might be able to sock away some money to cover the gap?"

"Yes. Yes, of course," I said, barely able to think straight.

How had everything come to this? I was a nice person, did my schoolwork, didn't bother anybody. How?

"Another thing, those boots of yours do look sort

of military," Ms. Fulham said. "Maybe talk to a recruiter? You know my daughter is a big fan of that TikTok singer, Bella… something. She was in the Navy, which of course has the GI Bill. And the National Guard has some very generous signing bonus offers. You could do your basic training during summer vacation and use the bonus money for tuition."

I shook my head politely. Talk about going from bad to worse. "No offense Ms. Fulham, but I doubt I'd get along with military style discipline."

"No worries, honey," she said, patting my hand. "I'll e-mail you, most likely tomorrow, with your counseling appointment."

I left the office, distraught, slowly crossing campus like I was on some sort of sick walk of shame. In my devastation, I was imagining that everyone who looked my way was inwardly laughing at me, enjoying the suffering they thought I so rightly deserved.

Poor little Jessa, got her pipes cleaned by three different men, and she now is broke.

With my luck, I'd get an offer for 'easy money' for college from some new creepy bastard. Could do the whole job on my knees, after all.

I'd rather go into the Marines.

I got back to my dorm room, closing and locking the door behind me. I hadn't seen Cole since the Spring Show, but that didn't mean I was ready to let my guard down. I slept with a box cutter under my pillow now because of him.

My phone rang, and I saw that it was Griff. "Hey there."

"Jessa? What's wrong?" he said, and his quiet concern cheered me, if only for a moment. He already knew me so well that he could hear the distress in my voice from a simple greeting. "Is it something with class?"

"Yes and no," I said, sighing.

"Say, I was calling to invite you for dinner. Mason got a recipe he wants to try, and I was hoping we could have a, you know, normal sort of dinner date? Or as normal as it gets for the four of us?"

I smiled, and for a moment considered telling him of my latest bad news. But I couldn't talk about it just yet. "Griff, that sounds lovely. But I'm not in a good place right now. I'm safe and all that, I just need some time to think. Can I get a raincheck?"

"Of course, beautiful. Are you sure you're okay?" Griff asked.

"Yeah, I promise. I was thinking of calling Birdie and Roxy for some girl time, you know?"

"All good, baby," Griff assured me. "Then maybe you and I meet up for morning coffee, say... eight thirty at the shop right by the arts building?"

"If we do that, we'll be seen."

"I know... and I don't care," he said. "You're more important, and people are going to find out eventually, anyway."

I thought it over for a second. "Sure. As long as you promise to buy me one of those breakfast croissants."

"Deal. Hey… if you need us, we're here for you. Have a good night."

Griff hung up, and I reflected on his words for a moment. They were there for me, and it helped. But I needed my girls.

I texted Roxy and Birdie a simple message… *Bat Signal.* I got replies quickly, and twenty minutes later Birdie flew in with Roxy in tow, one holding a double stack of pizzas, the other hoisting a backpack that could only contain beer from the way it rattled and sloshed.

"Slide over bitch, the 'zas are hot," Birdie said, setting down her armload before turning and going back to lock the door. "There. Now none of these beer hounds from the third floor will be able to barge in on our food or drink."

"Okay, Jessa, you sent up the signal," Roxy said, unzipping her bag to take out the first beer. "What the hell is up?"

I took a deep breath and drained half a beer before speaking. God, I needed this. "I've gotten myself in a bit of a problem," I said. "With Griff… and Indy… and Mason."

"Oh my *gawd!*" Birdie exclaimed while Roxy rolled her eyes. "And remind me who each of them are?"

"Griff Ledger, head of the art department. Indy Dawson, visiting scholar and art instructor. Mason Acker… comms professor."

"Okay, right," Roxy said. "When you go all in, you go

all in with quality, don't you? Those are three of the sexiest professors on campus!"

Birdie shot her the stink eye. "Hey now, I can think of another three who are pretty freaking hot!" she said. "But first things first. What's the problem?"

"You remember my fake boyfriend, Cole?" I asked.

"Duh," Roxy said. "I'm just waiting to give the man the beat down he deserves."

I should have let her loose on him ages ago. My bad.

"Turned out his bullshit wasn't all bluster. When I turned down his fucking psycho stalker proposal, he shanked me. Somehow over the past few weeks he figured out my secret, and narc'd me to my parents, who have now cut me off."

"Cut you off?" Roxy asked, and I nod. "As in—?"

"As in they told the university that they wouldn't pay my tuition and fees, and now I've got to pay my own way."

"Oh my god," Birdie said slowly, the gravity of what I'd said sinking in.

After a moment, Roxy spoke up. "And how are things with the guys, now that the shit has hit the fan?" she asked, throwing away her crust and reaching for another slice.

"Good. I think really good," I said, knowing I was underselling it. "Actually, things are great. I really... care for them. And I think they feel the same way about me. They invited me over the house tonight, but I needed to see my girls."

"Wait… they're *housemates?*" Roxy asked. "Top choice beef *and* convenient. Good lord. Well, keep going. Give us the deets on creepy Cole and the parents."

Over the two pizzas, I explained all the details. I even included some of the intimate ones at Roxy's request, and I had to admit it felt good to just talk about how amazing sex with each of my men was.

"It's like… food, I guess," I explained to a perplexed Roxy. "Look, these pizzas are good, right?"

"Right."

"But could you imagine eating the same pizza for dinner every night of your life? Like, that would be an imbalanced diet that would fuck up your body eventually. With the guys it's like I have… balance."

"I just… look, I know you two are both happy with the situation you're in, at least romantically," Roxy said. "But what about the reverse? Are they getting balance with just you, even as fucking awesome as each of you are?"

"I honestly don't know," I said. "I hope so. Roxy, Griff, Mason, Indy and I are just getting started."

"Me too," Birdie says. "Rox, I don't know what the future is bringing me and my guys. I'm hoping that we'll stick together, and that we'll always be tight regardless of where things take us. But that's what life is. Hoping for the best and moving forward."

Roxy took a deep breath, pursing her lips. "I guess. I just… I just can't see myself going down the same route you two have, that's all. Sure, there're some hot professors around, and yeah I've sat in class and imagined a few trysts. But to make it a reality, with three guys? I don't know if that's me. But I love you both, and I'll support you both no matter what."

"That's good, because it's Leo's birthday coming up, and I was thinking of giving him a big present," Birdie says. "I've had all my guys at once, so was thinking I could reverse it on him. You know, like two, maybe three girls on one guy? I bet he'd be all over that."

"*What?*" Roxy exclaimed, her eyes flying open. "You… you're serious?"

Birdie burst out laughing so hard she knocked over a full beer. "No, silly, but considering you didn't reject me right out of the gate tells me there's potential in you yet."

Roxy looked my way.

I patted her arm. "Let me get my head on straight with my own three guys before we start brainstorming about fancy birthday presents."

Roxy's mouth dropped open, and Birdie and I fell over, shaking with laughter.

20

GRIFF LEDGER

FINALLY, last day of class.

I'd already turned in my grades, of course, but we were in that hazy period where the university wanted to make sure the students didn't scatter to the winds before graduation day.

I rushed through my work for the day, feeling a combination of spring fever and anticipation. Mason was busy doing some final grading of papers, so it was left up to Indy and me as we put together an ad hoc party for our little foursome.

We had so much to celebrate.

We were able to get home early, followed by Mason, and it was right at six o'clock when I heard the familiar sound of Jessa's boots on the steps leading up to the porch, then the front door opening.

"Griff" she called. "I got your message. Indy... Mason? Why is it so dark in here—"

"Surprise!" we yelled when Jessa flipped on the lights to the living room and found all of us grinning.

"Oh my god!" she exclaimed, her hand on her chest. "What the hell... *Congratulations*? Congratulations for what?"

"Well," I said, reaching into my jacket and withdrawing an envelope. "I got this from the Dean's office today. They were going to notify you by e-mail, but I asked them to let me do it in person."

"What is it... oh my god. I... did I get it? Did I get it?" Jessa squealed, jumping up and down and opening the envelope and tearing out the letter inside.

My heart stopped for a moment as I watched happiness flood our beautiful girl's face.

"I got the scholarship!" she screamed at the top of her lungs.

"All on your own, I'd like to add," Indy said. "Remember, Griff had nothing to do with it."

"Bullshit," Jessa said, wiping tears away from the corners of her eyes. "I couldn't have done this without you. *All* of you."

We hugged and kissed her one at a time as Jessa got herself together. When we stepped back, I had to admit my own eyes were damp, too. "So... let's celebrate. And I get to fill you in on today's developments."

"Good or bad?" Jessa asked warily, smiling as she took a balloon Mason was holding and looped the string around her wrist.

"I think you'll be happy with most of the news," I said, leading her to the couch while Indy and Mason went to the kitchen, returning with champagne. "First off, I talked with the Dean about… us."

"Us?" Jessa asked, her face falling. "Why? What happened? Is there already a problem?" She looked from face to face, trying to ascertain what was up.

"No, I didn't have to. But, it was going to get out soon enough. Like with your roommate Birdie and her… arrangement, it might be an open secret, but it will become more public over time."

"I can handle it," Jessa said, and my heart flooded with pride.

"Good. Now, to begin with, the scholarship will pay your tuition," I said, "but not room and board, as you know. So you may have to leave the dorms."

"I… I figured," she said. "I already started looking for a cheap apartment. I'm sure I can find something."

"Damn right you can… right here in our house," I said, gesturing around. "Baby, you can stay here for as long as you want. Finish your Masters here, even."

Jessa looked around, smiling. "Really? I mean, sure, but… it'll be weird with Indy leaving and stuff."

All eyes turned in his direction.

"Actually, about that," he said, taking over, "that was another part of what Griff talked to the Dean about. After a few long discussions, I decided to take the summer off to do an eight week course on teacher training. Starting in August, you're looking at the newest associate professor of the arts department."

"You… but how? Why?" Jessa exclaimed. "I mean… Indy, you—"

"I did it because I learned a lot over the past weeks, thanks in large part to you, darlin'. I'd been gunning for a gallery deal for so long I forgot to take a look at my art objectively. Jessa, I'm good, but I don't have the talent you have. Your painting *Fulfillment* was greater than anything I could ever produce. Now, I'm not giving up, I'll still search for that piece inside me, but I think teaching is where I belong. I actually enjoy it more than I ever thought I would."

"Oh my god. So you're staying!"

She ran to throw her arms around him.

"One other thing, Jessa," Indy said. "I put in a call to a buddy who owns a gallery in the same city I'll be doing my teacher training. How'd you like to have a paid summer internship to go with that scholarship?"

Her mouth dropped open, and it wasn't until Mason reached out with a finger to lift her jaw back in place that she could talk again. "You... " she said breathlessly. "Just all of you... how can I... how do I put this?"

"Put it any way you want," Mason said. "A loss for words is not like you."

She nodded, and took a deep breath. "I... I love you. All of you. I've been thinking about it, about what's happened, and what it means. I've had a lot of talks with Birdie over the past few days, and even had lunch with her guys Cary and Leo. She's going out to Hollywood with the two of them for a series of business meetings and... well, that's their thing."

"And?" I asked quietly, waiting to hear everything on her mind.

"And I realized that I can't choose, not among you guys. I don't want to choose, I won't, and I never will. Now, this summer I might be with Indy most of the time, but maybe you and Mason could do a road trip every once in a while?"

I looked at my friends, who of course nodded. I reached out, taking Jessa's hand. "I love you too, Jessa. And yes, I think we can figure out some road trips. I mean, I'm a teacher, right? Aren't I supposed to get three months off a year to sit on my ass, at least according to some people?"

She laughed.

"I can't imagine being here at Wellshire without you," she added.

"Hell, I just need a good drawing model," Indy quipped as Jessa rolled her eyes. "Seriously though, this place is big enough for all of us."

"Well, with one alteration," Jessa said as she lifted her glass. "Griff, your summer homework is to figure out a way to get a mattress that all four of us can fit on when we want to."

"To bigger mattresses," I agreed, toasting, "and our amazing girl."

We went upstairs to my room, where we undressed Jessa and got down to the business of pleasing her. I woke up with her in my arms, Indy and Mason having gone back to their respective bedrooms after our last round of explosive orgasms.

"Good morning," Jessa whispered as she woke up, looking into my eyes. She'd fallen asleep with her head on my shoulder, and it was a feeling I looked forward to having on a regular basis. "I love you."

"I love *you*," I whispered back, giving her a kiss. "I'm going to have to redecorate this bedroom, look into a bigger bed. It was pretty funny last night when Indy and you fell off. Anyway, we'll figure it out. So are you happy, pretty lady?"

"God, am I," she said, humming. "Life's about perfect."

"What would make it more perfect?" I asked, and she shrugged.

"Well, I wish Cole didn't get away with his shit," she said. "And I wish Roxy could have happiness like we do. Like Birdie does. One guy, two guys, the whole football team… I don't care. I want her to know this warmth, this respect, this… love."

"That's what makes you so special, baby. And Roxy will find her match. Or matches, as the case may be. Now, as for Cole, I did have some good news on that, which I wanted to save so as not to mix with the purity of your achievements. He failed three of his classes. He's out of Wellshire. He was invited *not* to return."

"*What?* How?"

I shrugged. "Indy didn't give me the details, but apparently quite a few of his instructors gave him zeros on class participation this past semester. Character counts for something in a lot of instructors' books… and when it got out among the faculty that he'd harassed women, well, it pissed a lot of people off. If he hadn't flunked out, he would have been kicked out anyway. So, he's no longer your problem. He's no longer our problem"

"Wow. He just messed up his life, big time. Fuck that creep. Ding dong, the witch is dead."

Two minutes later, Jessa was using her lips and tongue in ways that I would never, ever get tired of. Watching her head bob up and down on my cock, I was in heaven, my eyes alternating between closing tight in pleasure and opening in utter amazement at what she was doing. "You like sucking me, babe?"

She pulled off, giving me a grin. "Griff, your girlfriend's a total oral ho. Giving and receiving."

"I may die of happiness."

She bent down again, but before her devilish lips could touch my engorged head, her phone buzzed with some sort of custom tone. "Oh, that's Roxy," she said, reaching to grab it. "No way… no *fucking way!*" she said, reading the screen.

"What?"

She put her phone down and returned to me. "Seems my bestie might have met an interesting guy."

"Nice. Must be something in the water."

Jessa reached out, taking my cock in her hand. "And get this. He's a professor."

Before I could say anything else, she swallowed me, and I was swept away by her oral skills.

All I knew was… good luck to whoever this other professor was.

He was going to need it.

EPILOGUE

It turned out Cole was in more trouble than Griff had let on. He was a disgusting predator on all levels, but he'd made a fatal mistake by going after an underage girl. Word had it, and I wasn't really interested, but the info just kept swirling around the campus gossip mill, that he was currently locked up. I had no idea how cases like his were handled, but he certainly was not going to have the cushy summer job at my dad's company like he'd once boasted he would.

Speaking of my parents, I didn't bother telling them about Cole. What good would it have done, to rub in their faces how poor their judge of character was? They were the way they were, and thank god I was not. My life had unlimited potential for happiness ahead, and if they didn't want to be part of that, well, I felt sorry for them.

Sometimes it's the people you love the most who also hurt you the most. It's a sad fact of life, but one I learned to accept the hard way. It stung. It always would. Like a scar you carry around. It fades, but never completely goes away. Like you need a reminder of how far you've come.

Indy and I had quite the 'summer of love,' where, for the most part, it was just the two of us except for the times Griff and Mason roadtripped to see us. That's when things heated up to an inferno, and I realized my love for each of them was only growing.

While Indy studied for his teacher training course every day, I puttered around in his friend's gallery, at first doing crap work—as I'd known to expect—like cleaning and packing things, and then, eventually getting to work with the artists and even the clients a bit. It was a perfect way to spend a mellow summer, which was just what I needed. I knew the upcoming semester was going to be a hell of a one. Now that I had a scholarship, the pressure was on more than ever for me to maintain my grades and produce top-notch artwork. But I was confident, especially because I had the support of the guys, and most importantly, my girls Birdie and Roxy, that I'd make it happen.

Griff, Indy, and Mason knew how important these women were to me, and offered to cover my dorm expenses so I had a place to hang with the girls when I needed it. I didn't expect to be there much, but it was a luxury to know I could get away when I wanted to.

Birdie and her guys, while all fulfilling their commitments to the university, were also working on a screen play based on one of the guys' books. I hadn't read it but I planned to, as soon as I finished my biography of Michelangelo. I'd heard it was really good.

Roxy was still kicking ass and taking names, trying to keep up with her coursework while taking all the shifts as a hotel maid that she could snag. She deserved all the credit that came her way. In a lot of ways, she was my hero, always powering through whatever shit life threw her way. So I was doubly excited for her when she started talking about a finance professor she had the hots for, and who seemed to have taken a liking to her, too.

Never thought I'd see the day when Roxy would break down and admit that professors—at least some of them— were hot as hell. Actually, I never thought I'd see the day when I had three of my own to go home to every night.

I had a feeling Roxy might be getting a taste of what I had. At least I hoped she did. There was nothing like it in the whole world.

I hope you loved reading this book as much as I loved writing it. Please visit my store to learn more about my books, and to buy directly from me! https://mikalaneshop.com/

Dear Reader:

I'm USA TODAY bestselling romance author Mika Lane, and am OBSESSED with bringing you sassy, steamy stories with imperfect heroines and the bad-a*s dudes they bring to their knees. I'll always bring you my signature humor and heat, topped off with a modern-day happily ever after.

My first book ever was *The Day I Ate the Milkyway*, a true fourth-grade masterpiece illustrated with crayons and bound with construction paper and glue. Nowadays, steamy romance gives purpose to my days and nights as I create worlds and characters that tickle the imagination. I live in magical Northern California with my own handsome alpha dude, sometimes known as Mr. Mika Lane, and two devilish cats named Chuck and Murray.

A dual citizen of the United States and Ireland, I have on more than one occasion spent my last dollar on a plane ticket somewhere, and am always planning my next escape. I often try new recipes on unsuspecting friends, search out hiding places to read undisturbed, and sadly kill every houseplant I bring home.

I LOVE to hear from readers when I'm not dreaming up naughty tales to share. Visit my online shop https:// mikalaneshop.com/ and say hello https:// mikalaneshop.com/pages/meet-mika.

xoxo, Mika